THE BLACK LORD

COLIN HINCKLEY

Cover Art by Matt Blairstone
Interior Illustrations by Echo Echo
Edited by Alex Woodroe

TENEBROUS

10p

PRESS

Published by Tenebrous Press.
Visit our website at www.tenebrouspress.com.

First Printing, September 2023.

Print ISBN: 978-1-959790-92-1
eBook ISBN: 978-1-959790-93-8

Cover art and design by Matt Blairstone.

Interior illustrations by Echo Echo.

Edited by Alex Woodroe.

Formatting by Lori Michelle.

Printed in the United States of America.

ALSO FROM TENEBROUS PRESS:

Dehiscent
a novella by Ashley Deng

House of Rot
a novella by Danger Slater

Agony's Lodestone
a novella by Laura Keating

Soft Targets
a novella by Carson Winter

Crom Cruach
a novella by Valkyrie Loughcrewe

Lure
a novella by Tim McGregor

One Hand to Hold, One Hand to Carve
a novella by M.Shaw

More titles at www.TenebrousPress.com

For Adam & Mariah,
Who knew better than to keep the windows open

The water showed him. The water showed him the hunger. A thick curtain was pulled around it; no one else was allowed to see. But the water had pulled it back to reveal the crackling, warm beauty that makes everything move. It showed him because he was special and he deserved to see. Even now, when the hunger is the only electricity able to contract his rotting muscles, he loves it. It swims sweet through his veins.

"The water is wide, I cannot cross o'er."
—*Scottish Folk Song*

I. THE TALL THING

EDDIE KNOWS WHAT his parents are fighting about. Even if it's about bills, or 'Dad's boozing' as Mom calls it, or what's for dinner—it doesn't matter. The fighting is always about Danny, even when it's not. Eddie knows this because they didn't fight before Danny was taken away. And he knows this because his parents don't look at each other for more than a few seconds anymore, and because at night Mom spoons him for twenty minutes before going upstairs to bed. Ever since Danny was taken, his parents feel like walking glass statues to him, and he's always wondering which one is going to break first.

He's sitting on the floor of his bedroom reading a book called *The Divine Comedy,* and he doesn't understand it. He thought because it had comedy in the title that the book would be funny and maybe it could distract him, if only for a little bit. But it turns out the story isn't funny at all. The drawings that accompany the story do fascinate him, but he's having trouble looking at them, let alone reading the confusing story. The sound of his mom and dad trying not to shout is making his stomach feel like a tight drum being wound tighter. And, every once in a while, Mom or Dad lose control and a word or two quivers sharply in the air for a moment, only to sink back down into the muted, angry whispers. 'Booze,' 'cops,' and his own name are some of the words that ping like radio signals.

A week ago, Mom went to Danny's room after she woke up and found his crib empty. They called the police, and the police came and looked all over the house as Eddie sat at the top of the stairs, watching the officers scratch their hair and shake their heads. Dad walked from room to room but didn't say anything; Mom kept crying and saying she wanted to talk to the chief of police. Everyone in the state looked for Danny. Mom and Dad say they're still looking for him, but the phone doesn't ring as much as it did in the beginning.

Eddie wishes it weren't autumn break. Watching Mom float around the house like a smiling ghost is too hard. And when his father comes home at night, his face looks like a skeleton and he drinks more than he used to. Eddie would rather have his teachers asking him if he was okay than deal with the walking shells his parents have left behind. And when he's alone, he misses Danny.

He sits below his bedroom window and lets the sunlight heat his back. It feels good, but it doesn't release the knot in his stomach. He turns the page to two men riding on the back of a dragon with a man's face. In the background, scary pointed rocks jut toward a grey sky. The image makes Eddie think of winter, but he isn't sure why. The thought of winter stirs a dormant memory and Eddie lets his brain take him there. He remembers carrying Danny through their backyard the winter after he was born, kicking thick snow as his brother looked around at the blinding white in total awe. His parents watched them from the porch, his father laughing about something Mom said as she took picture after picture with her phone. Eddie thinks those pictures are probably still somewhere on his mom's laptop. He remembers how small Danny felt beneath the layers and layers of insulation from the cold, how he could sense the fragility of his brother. He remembers feeling a fierce sense of pride at the brief moment he was allowed to be the guardian of something as delicate as Danny, and understanding love in a way he hadn't before. He turns the page to distract himself.

A lull in his parent's conversation makes Eddie lift his head. There's something odd about it, but he can't place it immediately. Why does his room sound strange? He listens, his head cocked, frowning, and then realizes what it is. The birds outside his window have stopped chirping. Eddie thinks about why that might be just as the comforting heat on his back is cut off. A shadow spills on the floor in front of him. He turns.

For a moment, Eddie can't see what's blocking the light. It looks like a tall man with a small head standing just behind the glass. The man is large enough that he blocks almost the entire window and as Eddie's eyes adjust, he can see that it's not a man at all. It has hair on some parts of its body, but a lot of it is covered in loose, drooping pink skin. Some of it is scabby. It has a face that looks like a sick dog and eyes like Eddie's uncle Evan, who Mom and Dad say went to jail for hurting kids. Eddie stands up, almost tripping over the open book, and wants to start screaming. But his mouth stays shut and he's not sure why that is.

The tall thing doesn't move. Its blue eyes are watery, bloodshot, and the air around its body ripples like the skin is boiling hot. Eddie can see the big tree behind the creature, distorted, wobbling, beckoning to him. For a moment, he thinks he knows something about what he's seeing, but it slips away to the back of his mind as fresh waves of terror slosh against his brain. He can hear his parents talking, their voices calmer now, but still undercut with a note of anxiety. Eddie wants to call out to them, to alert them that their first-born is in peril. But Eddie can't say a word, and the tall thing crinkles its mouth: a putrid smile. Even through the glass, Eddie can smell its breath, a smell like hot, spoiled meat, mixed with a lower scent that makes him think of the basement. Steam rises from either side of its mouth; the steam fogs the glass of the window. It raises its arm and it has hands like a man, only with longer fingers and nails that look like the claws of a wolf; yellowed and canine. It taps on the glass in a frantic little rhythm. *Tap tap tap tap tap tap.*

"Hello, Eddie," the tall thing whispers. Its voice is gravel and snapping twigs. It's panting and he watches as a thin strand of saliva drips from the corner of its mouth and disappears below the window frame. "I have your brother, Eddie. I have Danny." Eddie feels something catch in his chest and his racing heart doubles its pace. The tall thing stares at Eddie, unblinking, and continues to tap. "Don't you want to see your brother, Eddie?" Without meaning to, Eddie nods. The tall thing breathes in sharply, then splays an open palm against the window and brings its face to the glass, fogging it with its breath. *Tap tap tap tap tap tap.* "Then let me in, Eddie," it says as a grey tongue emerges from behind its lips and licks away spittle.

Its face reminds Eddie of a raccoon he once found in the woods. The creature had been stuck in a bear trap and Eddie saw that it had almost chewed through its own leg. When it saw Eddie, it screeched at him, and started scratching at the dirt, making frenzied little grunting sounds. Its paws had begun to bleed as it tried to claw itself toward Eddie.

"Open the window. And I'll bring you to your brother," the visitor says. Eddie tries to stop looking at the brilliant blue eyes of the thing in his window, but he is locked in place. He thinks of the monster he learned about in school with the snakes for hair. *Medusa.* "Let me in," it says. Its smile is gone now. Its lips are pulled back and its face is so close to the window its teeth click against the glass as it breathes in and out. "Let me in or I'll eat your brother and use his bones to smash this window open. And then I'll eat you." As it says this, a fresh stream of saliva issues from its mouth and drips down the fogged glass, making racing trails of spit in the steam.

Eddie hears the clicking of his mother's heels as they come down the hall and the horrible blue eyes shift, glancing over the top of Eddie's head; he feels something in his forehead go loose, like a wire suddenly snapping inside him. He whips his head to look around at his door just as his mother opens it. She has clearly just put on makeup, but Eddie can see the red rims of her eyes under the mascara. Eddie looks back to the window, but the tall thing is gone. The fog left by its breath fades until no sign of the creature remains, and he turns back to his mother, who looks concerned.

"Jesus, Eddie, are you alright? You look like you're going to be sick." She walks to him and puts the back of her hand to his forehead. When she touches him, Eddie begins shaking and his mother pulls back in surprise, then swoops down and enfolds him into her arms. Eddie can't stop shaking and his legs give out and the two of them crumple together to their knees. He feels the hitch in his mother's chest as she cries. Eddie wants to cry too.

Instead, he throws up down the back of his mother's dress.

✳ ✳ ✳

Dr. Amleth is the last doctor in town who will make house calls. Eddie thinks it's probably because he isn't very good at being a doctor and the only way to distinguish himself is to offer a service no one else does. But he's his mother's only option. Eddie refuses to leave the house after what he saw in the window for fear of being carried away like his brother. When his mother asks him why he won't leave the house, he lies and says he feels too sick to get out of bed. He knows adults and he knows that telling them he saw a monster in the window would be dismissed, and that he would be told to stop making things up and be forced out of the house. And since he's on break and not missing any school, his mother doesn't force the issue, but lets him stay in bed. Besides, his mother has other things to focus on. His father is rarely around. He goes to work early in the morning and doesn't return until well after Eddie's bedtime. And when he is around, he's quiet and smells like a hospital corridor.

Dr. Amleth sits on the edge of Eddie's bed and listens to his heart through a stethoscope while Eddie's mother hovers in the doorway, trying to smile. Eddie twitches every time the doctor moves the cold metal to different parts of his chest and every time Dr. Amleth mumbles, "hold still." After a time, he removes the stethoscope and pulls a thin box out of his bag. He opens it and takes out a thermometer.

"How old are you now, Eddie? Eight?"

"Nine," Eddie says, looking to his mother, who is staring at a corner of the carpet, nibbling on her thumbnail.

"My goodness, you're getting older every day!" The doctor smiles at his stupid joke and brings the thermometer to Eddie's mouth. "I remember being nine. Broke my arm after falling into a rock quarry. My mother said I was lucky to survive, that I only broke my arm. Never went back there, even after a flood filled the place with water. Kids would throw rocks and ride boats in it. Never swim, though. All the adults said the water was poison because of the mining." The thermometer beeps and Dr. Amleth pulls it out to check it. He scribbles something down on a clipboard with Eddie's name at the top, then puts the board back into his bag and rests his hands on his lap, smiling at Eddie. Eddie tries to smile back, but feels nervous. He glances at his window. The curtains are drawn and he wonders if anything is standing on the other side of the glass.

"How are you feeling, Ed?" he asks.

Eddie hates being called Ed. His mother knows this and he sees her shift out of the corner of his eye, ready to swoop in if Eddie gets petulant. But he has no desire to argue with the strange man in his bedroom.

"Sick," he says, unsure what else to say.

"Sick how?" the doctor asks, all smiles and patience. "In your tummy? In your head? In your chest?"

"All of it, I guess," he replies. This isn't entirely false. Ever since Danny was taken, he's felt some combination of all three. And every time he thinks of Danny with the thing outside his window, fresh waves of sickness wash over him and he has to will himself not to vomit. "My stomach hurts, and my head hurts if I . . . if I think too hard." Dr. Amleth nods and Eddie sees understanding in his eyes.

"If you think about Danny?" he asks. The kindness in his voice surprises Eddie and he suddenly finds himself on the verge of tears. He looks down at the book on his lap. It's open to an image of a naked man with the head of a bull writhing on rocks as two men watch below. The image blurs as his eyes water and a tear plops audibly onto the paper. He feels Dr. Amleth pat his knee and stand up. He hears the doctor's bag snap shut and the sound of his feet on the carpet as he approaches the door.

"This isn't uncommon," he hears the doctor say to his mother. He attempts to keep his voice quiet, but Eddie still hears. "Often when a child loses a sibling, the grief can manifest itself physically. A sort of grief sickness. It can happen to anyone, but kids as young as Eddie are more susceptible. I'd say keep him occupied. Don't let the, uh, the absence of Danny invade his life too severely. Otherwise, he'll remain in the state that he's in." He pauses. "He'll get better once . . . once there's a more definitive answer. Right now, things are likely very amorphous and frightening for him." Eddie closes the book and rolls onto his side, his back to the adults. He doesn't want them to see his tears. He hears the shifting of fabric as his mother straightens her cardigan and likely crosses her arms, her classic "excuse me?" stance.

"I'm sorry, doctor. How am I supposed to keep the fact that his brother is missing from him?"

"I'm not saying to keep it from him," the doctor says, calm. "I'm saying don't make it the center of his life. If it's all he thinks about he's going to remain sick. And I imagine the last thing you need right now is for your child to be vomiting at all hours." His mother doesn't respond to this and Eddie feels the bubbling desire to tell her about the tall thing. He doesn't want his mother to pretend everything is fine. The thought of her walking around the house smiling and laughing is somehow so much worse than her quiet ghostly presence floating from room to room. But he says nothing. Instead, he closes his eyes and tries to force himself to sleep. The doctor and his mother exchange pleasantries, and he hears Dr. Amleth leave the room. After a time, the door clicks shut and his mother's heels clip-clop on the hardwood. He tries not to think of Danny.

As the sky darkens, Eddie swirls in and out of consciousness. Half-concocted images and stories ebb and flow across his mind; some are pleasant or neutral in their banality, but most are frightening. He sees his brother in a dark, damp hole, screaming as the sound of heavy breathing swells. An image of Dr. Amleth standing outside his window, his face pressed against the glass, fogging it with his breath. He sees the tall thing holding his brother in one hand, crouching in the dug-out hollow of a tree. As he watches, the thing opens its mouth with a loud click and its bottom jaw drops to its patchy, pink chest. Just as he brings the screeching baby to its open maw, Eddie's eyes shoot open and he barely suppresses a scream.

For a few moments, all he can hear is the throbbing of his panicked heart and all he can see is the darkness of his room. Something brought him from the depths of sleep. It ticks around the corners of his subconscious, and as the image of his brother about to be eaten dissipates, he hears it. The incessant tapping. *Tap tap tap tap tap tap.* The sound of nail against glass. He focuses his eyes on the window, which is covered by cream-colored curtains that look ghostly in the darkness. It's loud. It's not a quiet tap, not a gentle reminder at his window. It's the sound of something demanding to be seen.

Eddie doesn't move for a long time. Instead, he sits up in bed, the blanket pulled up and tucked around his neck so that he resembles a blanketed Christmas tree. The tapping continues unabated, and Eddie does his best to breathe deeply, to not let the screams out. He can feel them in his stomach, like mice in a burlap sack, tumbling over each other, desperate to leap out. But he knows, somehow, that a scream will be the end of it. He knows, without pulling back the curtain, that he is receiving a warning. Then, barely audible beneath the horrible tapping:

"Eddie," it says, its voice thin and excited. "Let me see you, Eddie."

All at once, Eddie feels that wire in his forehead go taut. A little whimper escapes his mouth as he drops the blanket and starts crawling toward his window. His neck strains, trying to pull himself backward, back to the pillow and the blanket, back toward safety. But his body crawls, nothing more than human-shaped meat—Eddie, with hopeless revulsion, understands this horrible truth for the first time in his young life—moving obediently, beyond his control. His mind, tumbling over itself in confusion and terror, cannot comprehend why his hand is reaching for the curtain and pulling it away. But it is, and he does.

In the blue moonlight, the tall thing stands. It breathes in a ragged rhythm, its pink chest shining, raw skin gooey and exposed to the night, inflating and deflating like something mechanical. Its face is pressed against the window, clouding it, and its eyes are locked on Eddie, as if it had been tracking his position all along, even through the curtains. Eddie recoils and nearly falls off the bed but catches himself and instinctively pulls his blanket around his shoulders as he shimmies back to his pillow. The tall thing watches him, both of its hands pressed hungrily against the window, its breathing somehow intensifying.

"Open up, Eddie," it says, all breath and saliva. It licks its lower lips and presses itself harder against the window. Eddie can hear the glass creaking in the frame. "Your brother misses you. He talks about you, Eddie. He says, 'Where's Eddie? Where's my brother?'" The thing grins, as if making an irrefutable point. Its grey tongue, like a piece of spoiled meat, emerges to lick the window frame, as if trying to taste Eddie through the glass. Eddie inhales, gathering as much of himself as possible while his mind stutters like a cog tangled in rope.

"Danny's only one," he says, his voice barely audible, even to himself. "He can't talk yet." Then, after a moment's consideration, Eddie forces the muscles in his face to shift, so that he is staring into the electric blue eyes of the monster. He can already see the rage. "Liar," he whispers.

Seconds pass and the thing doesn't move. It merely breathes, its horrible front teeth clicking against the glass as it inhales and exhales. Eddie thinks of the raccoon he left for dead in the woods.

He wonders if the skeleton is still where he left it to die.

Then, the thing's lower jaw drops. Eddie knows what's going to happen a moment before it does and he snatches up his pillow and pulls it over his head, pressing his hands over his ears. But that's not enough to shut out the horrible screech that emits from the tall thing. A sound like metal dragged against slate, the thing screams at Eddie, its eyes bulging in lunatic fury. The sound feels like it's ripping Eddie's room in two, like Eddie himself is being torn down the middle. The air around the thing's mouth vibrates, then turns black, as if the sound is darkness, leeching from deep inside its stinking gullet. It fills everything, turning every shadow into a bottomless pit, his normal, familiar things—his bureau, his bookcase, the picture of his family, still intact—winking out like fireflies yanked into a toad's mouth. The room shrinks, closing the gap between Eddie and the thing at his window. He feels himself slipping, slipping away as the tall thing presses its whole body against the glass and even over the sound of the thing's rage, he can hear the glass about to give. And then the darkness swallows him.

✳✳✳

Eddie thinks he might be dead. He remembers the tall thing at the window, its terrible screeching. He's relieved that he doesn't remember being eaten, though. He wonders if he'll get to see Danny now that he's dead; he's pretty sure the tall thing lied to him about his brother still being alive. The thought makes his chest hurt, which strikes him as odd. Because, of course, dead people don't have pains in their chest.

Then, he hears birds singing. As he swims from the bottom of his consciousness, red-orange sunlight bleeds through his eyelids. He can feel its warmth. He cracks one eyelid, then the other. His room is flooded with morning light. It looks the same. His windows are shut tight, intact, and the curtain closest to him is pulled back so that he can see the massive maple growing out back, ripples of wind pulling at its branches. He's tangled in his sheets and quilt, the blankets wrapped around him like a toga. His pillow is damp with sweat. Eddie twists his head around so that he can see the alarm clock by his bed. It's 8:38. It's a Saturday, so his parents will be home. His father is probably sleeping and his mom is likely out running errands.

Eddie tugs the blankets off him, rolling over to unspool the slightly damp sheets from his body. Had his confrontation with the tall thing been a dream? After all, that screeching was loud enough to wake the whole neighborhood, yet at no point does he recall his parents coming to check on him, let alone the police coming to investigate the strange sound emanating from the home of a missing child.

But the tall thing must have done strange things to him. He remembers the feeling of losing control, of being compelled to pull back the curtain despite his rational mind trying to desperately yank him away. Maybe only Eddie can hear the tall thing. Maybe the tall thing can decide who hears it. He glances at the window. It doesn't look any different. There are no cracks in the glass, no smudges that he can see. But just looking at the window gives him a sense of queasy anticipation, as if at any moment, the thing's head will slowly rise into view, blue eyes locked on Eddie.

This thought propels Eddie out of bed and he does a skittish little half jog out his bedroom door and into the hallway, forcing himself not to take one last peek back at his window. As he walks into the kitchen, he tilts his ear, listening for any sound of his parents. But the house is silent. Sunlight glistens off the soapy dishes left in the sink from last night's meal. A fly buzzes from a pot crusted with tomato sauce to a plate with a petrified noodle stuck to its surface. Suddenly hungry, Eddie goes to the cabinet in search of cereal. He finds it mostly bare, save for a few spices and an open box of rice pilaf. The fridge yields similar results. His empty kitchen drops a hot rock of pain into his stomach that has nothing to do with hunger. Not knowing what else to do, Eddie climbs onto the stool in front of the marble counter and lowers his head. The tears come quickly. Hot and merciful, they release the knot in his stomach and he cries softly in the empty kitchen with only the buzzing of the fly to keep him company. It's in this moment that Eddie understands for the first time how lonely it is to be alive.

After a time, he stops crying. His eyes hurt and he shifts his head so that he is resting his cheek against his arm. He watches the fly buzz from pot, to plate, to the window above the sink, and back to the pot. The buzzing is welcome, cutting the silence in the kitchen into manageable chunks that he can take one at a time. He hears a thump upstairs.

Eddie lifts his head and listens. There's the familiar sound of his father's heavy footsteps as the floorboards creak beneath his weight. He expects the sound to travel across the floor to the bathroom, but instead the sound comes toward him and stops right above his head. For a moment, Eddie is puzzled. He knows the layout of his parent's bedroom, and knows there's nothing in that corner. Then he hears the muffled sound of his father's voice and realizes he's made a call from the upstairs telephone. His voice is urgent, but controlled, and the sound of it surprises him. Over the past week, he's barely talked at all, except to fight with mom or exchange brief greetings with Eddie. This was the voice of his father he recognized from a little over a year prior, when Danny was on the way and his parents kept getting calls from a land developer trying to buy their house. His father had explained to Eddie that a real estate company wanted to buy up all their land and their neighbors' land so they could build condominiums, which would have meant cutting down all the trees and leveling all the houses. His father had led the fight against the deal, organizing all the neighbors and convincing them not to sell to the company. He had spent most of his evenings on the phone with lawyers, neighbors, and people from the real estate company; his voice was always confident and firm. Eddie and his mother would sit at the counter, precisely where Eddie is sitting now, and pretend not to listen to his father's quiet commanding voice flowing down the stairs. Whenever his father would raise his voice to talk over whoever was on the other line, Eddie would watch his mother's face as she smiled a fierce, tight little smile. Her eyes would glow like moonlight, and in those moments, Eddie loved his family so much that it made him shake. This is what his father sounds like now.

Eddie slips off the chair and goes to the bottom of the stairs. His father's voice has stopped, save for an occasional "uh-huh" or "no, not yet." Eddie studies the stairs, which are carpeted in ugly orange shag. He knows these stairs very well, knows which ones squeak and where. He lifts his foot and soundlessly begins climbing. His father has resumed speaking, and Eddie listens as he ascends.

"I don't know. It's entirely possible, but I haven't seen much of him. He spends most of his time in his room . . . yes . . . yes, but the doctor seems to think it's just a byproduct of . . . of the circumstances we're in . . . no, I haven't . . . Look, if that's the case, then it's a lot more serious than . . . okay. Yes, okay. But this isn't like last time . . . yes, but I haven't *seen* anything . . . yes. You do too, right? Like every night? At least since Danny . . . well, then maybe you need to talk to him, Mom. After what happened . . . "

Eddie has reached the third step from the top and comes to a halt. His father is talking to his Grandma Sandy. Eddie hasn't seen her since the first day Danny went missing when she had come to help look and make food for the search party. They had seen a lot of Grandma Sandy after Danny was born. She was always coming by with odd concoctions she had made for Danny, homemade baby food that he seemed to love. But she hasn't returned since those first couple days, and Eddie hasn't even thought of her since then. He climbs the last two steps, puts his back to the wall next to the doorway, and listens.

"Okay. Can you come this afternoon? I think he's sleeping now . . . Should I . . . ? Okay. But, Mom, what if . . . yeah. No, I think she's on a run? No, I know, you're right, as usual."

Eddie chances a glance around the corner and sees his father sitting on the bed, the phone pressed hard against his ear. His face is covered in stubble, but his eyes are clear and he's dressed in a button-down shirt and khakis. A half empty bottle of Jack Daniels sits between his feet. As Eddie peers around the corner, his father lifts his head and makes direct eye contact with Eddie, whose stomach does an instinctual lurch at being caught eavesdropping. But instead of a swift reprimand, his father smiles as if he's the one who's been caught. He gestures for Eddie to come into the room, which Eddie does, confused and desperately curious.

"Mom, I have to go. Someone just walked in the room . . . Yes. Yes, it is . . . I will. See you in a few hours . . . love you, too. Bye now." His father pushes the disconnect button on the receiver and lets the phone dangle in his hand. He looks up at Eddie, his face no longer smiling. He pats the spot next to him on the bed.

"Come sit down, Eddie. We have a lot to talk about."

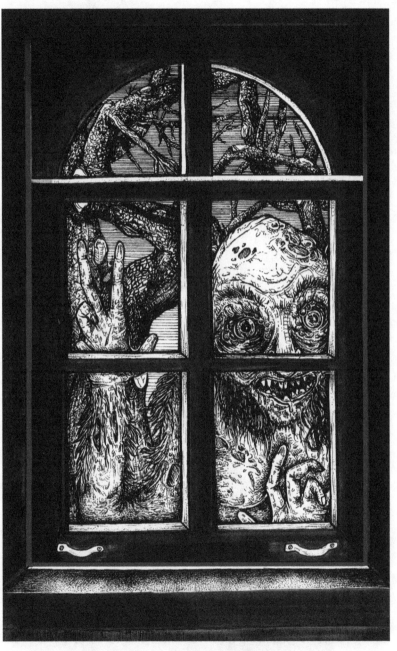

"Let me in or I'll eat your brother and use his bones
to smash this window open. And then I'll eat you."

II. THINK OF A MOUNTAIN

L AURA REACHES DOWN to touch her son's pale, wide-eyed face, and watches him erupt into horrifying shaking. Her heart lurches; she swoops down, and grips him tightly, feeling his stomach contract as warm vomit oozes down her back. She enfolds him tighter, trying not to gag. She lifts him from the floor, momentarily stronger than she actually is, and lays him down on his bed, angling herself carefully so as not to let the bile on her back slide off and hit the floor or him. When she pulls away after laying him down, she sees that he's crying. He keeps saying "I'm sorry, mom," over and over, his nose runny and his mouth caked in puke. With every tearful apology, a new crack appears in her already splintered heart.

"Hush, hush now, Eddie," she says, pulling up the blanket and trying to smile, failing. "You lie down now and I'm going to get cleaned up. Then I'm going to call Dr. Amleth and we'll get you better, okay?"

"I'm sorry, momma," he says again, wiping away tears and bile in equal measure.

"It's okay, baby. I'll be right back." She runs out into the hallway and snatches the cordless phone on her way to the basement. She strips off her dress as she goes, letting out a quiet sob every few steps, but refusing to let the despair take her. At the bottom of the stairs, she throws the soiled dress into the giant industrial sink next to the washer, then goes to phone the doctor.

Once the appointment is made, she hangs up the phone and nearly throws it into the basement corner. Instead, Laura picks up the sponge, turns on the water, and scrubs at her dress, trying not to cry. She is so goddamn sick of crying that when she feels the now all-too-familiar loosening in her chest, she squeezes her wrist and grits her teeth until it recedes. Crying isn't going to bring Danny home and it sure as hell isn't going to help Eddie.

As she stands in front of the sink, realizing the dress is ruined, she breathes in deeply and thinks of a mountain. It's a trick she learned from a self-help book called *The Way Forward: Managing Grief through Metaphor*. The mountain is supposed to center her, make her feel grounded as she thinks of something strong and unchanging. She pictures Mt. Fuji, floating above the clouds, imposing and perfect in its purple grace.

It doesn't help.

She stands in her bra and underwear, feeling exposed and cold. It's only early autumn, but the subterranean basement is frigid. She rubs her arms, trying to warm herself. The doctor said he would be there around three, which gives her enough time to compose herself and clean Eddie up. But in this moment, Laura genuinely doesn't know what to do. She knows she should leave the dress—her favorite, a nice green and red floral—to soak in the sink, go upstairs and get dressed, check on Eddie and make sure he doesn't vomit again, then call Todd, who has taken the car somewhere to cool off. He has decided to skip work today, which is what set their argument off to begin with. Laura tried, calmly, to explain to him that they couldn't afford for him to take a day off, that every cent counted now. But his response, as it always seemed to be since that day, was that he needed time to himself. To grieve privately. This is what stings Laura the most. She has tried to tell him, in so many ways, that she is drowning. That she needs something, anything to cling to. But instead, he took the station wagon and drove off to God knows where, most likely to drink. And now she's standing in her basement in her underwear, unable to comprehend the very thought of going upstairs to face her son.

But she squeezes her wrist, grits her teeth, and gives herself a quick, sharp slap in the face. She sees stars for a moment, then steadies herself on the edge of the sink. After she has controlled her breathing, she pushes herself back, turns smartly, and trots up the stairs to get dressed.

✳✳✳

Laura leans in the doorway of her Eddie's room as Dr. Amleth examines him.

She's biting on her thumbnail, a habit Todd has always pointed out as gross, and tries to give Eddie encouraging smiles. The doctor has taken his temperature and is scribbling on his clipboard and Eddie is looking at the cream curtains covering the window with an expression that Laura doesn't recognize from him. She too directs her attention to the window, but sees nothing out of place. She looks back at Eddie. He looks so much older than he should. She hears Amleth ask how he's feeling.

"Sick," he says. He looks lost and tired and Laura feels the profound urge to push the foolish doctor out of the way and hold her son, to tell him everything will be fine. That his father will come home and stop drinking. That they'll find Danny, scared but safe. And that any day now, they'll reclaim their lives and continue to live as they were supposed to. She resists the temptation and continues to chew on her thumb. The doctor asks him with well-practiced patience where specifically he feels sick. Eddie tells the doctor that his stomach hurts and so does his head. The doctor smiles.

"When you think about Danny?" he asks softly. Laura straightens up, alarmed. She almost says something; about how he has no business forcing Eddie to talk about his brother, about the fact that he's a medical doctor and isn't here to calibrate Eddie's mental health. But then she sees the surprised look on Eddie's face, followed by a quick contortion of his mouth. A single tear drops from his face onto the book he's reading. She recognizes the Doré drawing and realizes he's reading *The Divine Comedy*. She briefly wonders how he managed to get his hands on it. The doctor pats Eddie's leg and stands up. Laura watches her son as the doctor walks toward her. Eddie looks like he's been punched in the gut. She turns her attention to the doctor, his face serene and untroubled. She gets the overwhelming urge to smack him for basically leveling her son.

He tells her Eddie's experiencing what he calls "grief sickness." That it's common and she shouldn't worry. He says something about keeping him occupied, about not letting Danny be "the center of his life." She watches her son as he closes his book—that strange look still on his face—and rolls over onto his side, facing away from them. He reminds her of a baby armadillo, rolling into a ball to protect himself from danger. She crosses her arms and grips her bicep, trying to keep her voice level.

"I'm sorry, doctor," she says, whipping up a deadly smile. "How am I supposed to keep the fact that his brother is missing from him?" The doctor gives her some bullshit answer that basically boils down to "it's psychosomatic, your son's not actually sick," and she doesn't respond. Instead, she looks at her son's back and thinks of a mountain. The doctor says he'll see himself out and walks out of the room.

Laura lingers in her son's doorway. Eddie is a smart boy. It's something that she's fiercely proud of. He's always been miles ahead of the other kids in his age group, taking up reading for pleasure by the age of six and reading novels by the age of eight, pulling anything he could off the shelf, *The Lord of the Rings, Something Wicked This Way Comes,* and once, alarmingly, 'Salem's Lot, which Laura had hastily plucked from his hands, promising he could read it when he was older.

Laura is deathly afraid that her son's bright light will be extinguished. The circumstances surrounding Danny's disappearance are so strange, so unnerving, that she's worried she'll never truly be able to make sense of it herself, let alone Eddie. Watching him now, as he lays in the fetal position on his bed, she has the distinct feeling that he's keeping something from her. That he has some crucial piece of information that he's not sharing. Laura desperately wants to know what he's thinking. She desperately wants to tell him that he doesn't need to keep anything from her.

Instead, she turns around and walks to the kitchen and forces herself to think about what to make for dinner.

✳ ✳ ✳

Laura is standing at her bureau, trying not to move. The top drawer is open, one white sock draped over the edge like the lolling tongue of a dead beast. A pack of Marlboro Reds lies crumpled in the corner, the package slightly open so that she can see the rows of light-brown filters, like stained teeth in a red mouth. Next to it, partially obscured by the cigarettes, is a photograph. She can see Danny's face, locked in an ecstatic shriek of glee, the left side of his face covered in white frosting. Eddie stands next to him, both of his hands gripping his brother's high chair for dear life and his head thrown back in a laugh so powerful that he's barely able to keep his balance. And she sees herself, hovering on the other side of Danny, a plastic fork in one hand and a smashed piece of vanilla cake in the other. She is trying not to laugh. She is failing.

In one fluid motion, Laura reaches in, snatches the pack of cigarettes, and snaps the drawer shut with her other hand. She flicks open the pack and pulls out a cigarette after three attempts to lock her thumb and forefinger around one of the filters. She sticks it in her mouth and walks to Todd's bureau, scanning the top for a lighter. His bureau is bare except for a belt and a tiny carving of a fox his mother gave him two Christmases ago, so she goes downstairs to light it off the stove.

Walking down the stairs in the dark, she pictures Danny as he looks at her from his highchair, a piece of yellow cake in front of him. He smiles at her, mischief in his eyes, then plunges his face into the dessert with a squeal. She grips the railing and tries to think of how good the smoke is going to feel in her lungs. Instead, she sees Eddie as he rears back and lets out a deep, beautiful belly laugh—a man's laugh—and she pulls her hand from the railing and smacks both sides of her face. Stars blossom in the darkness.

It is well past midnight. Todd has been gone for nearly nine hours without so much as a text. Eddie has been in bed since eight thirty. She has just finished watching a movie about aliens, trying to stay awake, wanting to see the look on Todd's face when he discovers he can't slip into bed and sleep off his drunkenness while she dreams of their son. But even in the state she's in, she's having trouble keeping her eyes open. The pair of slaps has momentarily brought her into lucidity and away from thoughts of her family. She's looking forward to that first drag.

She walks on the balls of her feet across the kitchen, not wanting to wake Eddie. The stove is gas powered and after clicking for a few moments, the flame whooshes to life. Carefully, she dips her head and lights the end of the cigarette in the open flame, enjoying the heat on her face. She snaps off the burner and trots to the front door, moving quickly so as not to leave any smoke residue in the house, and opens the front door out onto the porch.

The night air is stagnant and cold. The sky is cloudy and she can make out no stars. The moon is only a dim smudge over the horizon. She wraps her arms around her torso, cursing herself for not grabbing a cardigan. Walking to the edge of the porch and leaning against the wooden railing, she stares off into the woods and pulls on her cigarette. Immediately, she begins coughing and almost drops it on the ground, the smoke searing her lungs. She pulls the crook of her elbow up to her mouth, trying to stifle her cough, suddenly aware and uncomfortable at how loud she is in the darkness.

She gets her breathing under control and takes another tentative drag. This one is better, and her head swims with the comfortable warmth of nicotine. She sighs, exhaling hot smoke, and stares blankly into the woods. The shadows are still, but the night is alive with sound. Crickets sing to each other, bats shriek above her, and the forest drops leaves and branches under the weight of small, nocturnal creatures. It's comforting, in an eerie sort of way. Laura spent most of her professional life in New York, and standing on the fire escape smoking a cigarette and listening to the city had been one of her most private and favorite things about living there. The city was ceaseless in its noise, and that was another kind of comfort. As constant as the ground beneath her feet. When she had fallen in love with Todd, and they had devised their plan to move to Vermont and build a life, she had been apprehensive, bordering on terrified, thinking of the vast silence that their new pastoral existence would bring. She needn't have worried. Though it's an altogether different collage of sound, the countryside turned out to be just as noisy as the city. Even in the cold November, the forest teems with the sound of nature. Constantly percolating in conversation with itself.

A memory, clear and unexpected as a punch to the gut, flashes across her mind. Her family, sitting together on the deck, enjoying one of their late summer outdoor dinners as the sun drifted lazily toward the horizon. Danny sat on Eddie's lap and Todd drank a beer as they watched a smattering of turkey vultures circle something about a half mile off. Danny cooed and pointed, and Eddie enunciated *"vul-chur"* for his little brother, as if he could learn the word and repeat it back to him.

"They got the scent of something," Todd said, with the calm certainty of a scientist, and took another sip of beer. Laura was drinking a glass of wine and made a scoffing sound. She gently tugged on his earlobe, their secret teasing gesture.

"Please, tell us more, professor," she said. Todd swatted away her hand, but he was smiling.

"Why do they circle like that?" Eddie asked, as Danny burbled and squealed on his knee.

"Well," Todd said, and gave Laura a smirk. He tugged on his shirt as if straightening the lapels of a lab coat. "They're looking for predators that might be waiting to pounce on them when they're eating. They go around and around," he spun his finger in a tight circle, "looking for danger. And only when they're sure it's safe . . . " He turned suddenly and swooped Danny out of Eddie's arms and buried his face in his tummy, like he was a vulture devouring decaying flesh. Danny squealed with surprise and delight and Eddie laughed and Laura laughed and soon the whole family was laughing. Above them, in the dying summer light, the vultures circled, waiting for their moment.

Laura cocks her head. She's been pulled out of her reverie, though at first she's not sure why. Something shifted while she was caught up in the painful, sweet memory; but her brain, still strained from grief and the constant low-grade terror, can't quite grasp it.

A moment later, she has it, and takes an involuntary step back, the cigarette forgotten in her limp fingers.

The night is silent. There are no crickets, no softly crashing branches or flitting bats. Laura's white breath billows in front of her, thundering in the new silence. The darkness is close to complete at the forest's edge. The porchlight casts a weak, ashen glow onto the lawn and driveway, but it doesn't penetrate the shadows. Laura strains her eyes, trying to peer through the smoke and the cold and the dark.

The grass, nearly dead, runs right up to the tree line, then stops abruptly and turns to soil, leaves, and pine needles. A gust of wind rustles the trees, loud as sirens in the night. Her eyes are pulled to a gap between two maple trees. The trees stand no more than three feet apart. The darkness between them is thick, impenetrable. Laura has the sensation of looking at a very deep pool of water, its surface still as death. Hiding something.

The more she stares, the more she thinks she can see something. A silhouette. A form. Shadow against shadow. She doesn't move. She waits.

A puff of white breath blossoms between the trees, then evaporates.

Laura drops her cigarette and turns. She runs into the house and slams the door behind her, not thinking of her sleeping son. She locks it, then presses her ear against the wood. Outside, she can hear the chirrup of crickets, and the wind in the trees. She places a hand over her eyes and turns so her back is against the door. She slides until she's sitting and tries to decide whether to laugh or cry. She settles on weeping silently in the cold, dark foyer of her home.

✳✳✳

At almost two in the morning, she hears the front door open and close, quieter than usual. Instead of bumping into things and making a racket, Todd walks swiftly and quietly from the front door, to the bottom of the stairs, up the steps, and then there he is, standing in their bedroom door. He doesn't look the least bit surprised to see her sitting up in bed, waiting for him. Even more unexpected, he looks stone cold sober. He looks the way he did before Danny disappeared: solid, clear. Despite her surprise, she folds her arms and settles into her disappointed/expectant stare, a look she knows she's good at. But he doesn't crumple and avert his eyes like he often does. No, this time he walks to the edge of the bed and climbs into it, keeping eye contact the entire time. He maneuvers himself so he's sitting cross-legged in front of her. This is the most directly he's looked at her since Danny disappeared and she is knocked completely off balance.

"I'm sorry," he says. She blinks at him and she can feel the hardness built up over the last couple weeks melting. Immediately, she resents him for it. For taking away the anger so quickly, the only thing that felt good anymore. But she doesn't unfold her arms. He sets his mouth in a perfect line, the precursor to a speech, likely rehearsed. "I know how bad I've been. I've been hiding from you, and I've seen how hard you're trying to pull me out of my hole. I'm done with that now." He tries to smile, but it looks like it hurts him. "I'm done with the boozing. It's not good for us, it's not good for Eddie." Here, the smile drops and he reinforces his intense gaze. She is struck, as she always is, by his eyes. So blue.

"Things are going to get worse before they get better. There are ... there are things you don't know about my family, Laura. And it looks like they've come into play." Again, she simply blinks at him. What is he talking about? The only family he has left is his mother, and she's totally unremarkable in personality or disposition. Is he talking about his father? Or his pervert brother? During the course of their relationship, Todd had mentioned them maybe two times. And both occasions were to draw negative comparisons. Finally, she unfolds her arms and grips him gently by the shoulders.

"Todd. Can you just please be straight with me? What the hell are you talking about?"

Now he averts his gaze, escaping to his side-eye refuge. "I know this is hard to understand, but I can't talk about it right now. Tomorrow. Tomorrow we can talk about—"

Something in the room changes. A sudden thickness; Todd's head jerks and she knows he feels it too. Laura feels something in her stomach turn sideways. Sickness washes over her and she thinks she can hear a high-pitched squealing sound, just at the peak of her auditory perception. She doubles over, holding her stomach, then whips up her head just in time to see Todd's boot disappear down the stairs. Something is very, very wrong, and using all the strength she can, she throws off her blankets and tumbles out of bed. She runs to the stairs and hurtles down them thinking, *Not Eddie, not Eddie, please, please, not Eddie.* There's nothing concrete to be frightened of, but the feeling in her gut is so strong, she cannot deny it. She hits the landing hard, hurting the bottoms of her feet, but she doesn't slow. She tears around the corner and sees her husband standing in their son's doorway, one hand placed on the doorjamb.

No. She thinks. *No, no, no, no, no, no.* She sprints down the hall as Todd turns and puts a finger to his lips. Surprised, she stops running just before she collides with him. He holds out a hand and grabs her shoulder to steady her. He gives her an anxious little smile.

"It's okay," he whispers. "Look." He gestures into the room and she peers around him to see. Eddie is asleep. He's somehow twirled himself up into his sheets and he looks like he's sweating a little. Hopefully, that's just the sickness breaking. Laura sighs deeply, putting one hand to her chest and the other on the small of Todd's back. He puts his arm around her shoulder and pulls her in, which is the single most comforting gesture Todd has made in a week. She thinks of a mountain.

Her gaze is pulled away from Eddie. Her eyes feel like ball bearings dragged by a magnet, and she finds herself looking at the window. One cream curtain is pulled aside, and Laura can just see the maple out back. Suddenly, she very deeply wishes to open the window—to let the cool night air (*letmein,eddie*) into her son's room. She feels her legs moving forward, and then stops. Not because she wants to. She wants nothing more than to cross the room and throw the window open, she's never wanted anything more in her life, and it's like a fever, that window needs to be open, her son needs fresh (*meatfreshmeat*) air and it needs to be opened *now now now* but something is holding her back, why isn't she moving, she looks around and Todd is holding her by the shoulders and he's saying something what is he saying what is the bastard fucking saying can't he see she needs

"LAURA."

to open that window?? If she can't get to that window, she'll be in so much trouble, she'll be in so much trouble and why won't

"*LAURA.*"

he let her go? Let her . . .

He's holding the sides of her face, too hard, and looking into her eyes.

"Laura. Laura, listen. Look at me. You're not going to open the window. Look at me." Those blue eyes.

"Laura, baby, listen to me. Listen to my voice. It's Todd. Stop struggling."

She stops. His hands feel good against her face. Warm, strong. She looks at him and she can see him now. What was she doing? She was going to open the window? Why would she do that? After she left it open that night . . . she thinks she's about to know something, but then it skitters away. Her husband speaks.

"Okay, Laura. Here's what I need you to do. You need to go upstairs. Get the earplugs out of your drawer. Put them in, then go to sleep. Can you do that?"

She realizes, all of a sudden, that she is immensely tired. "Okay," she says. A little pinprick of fear pokes her in the chest. "Todd. Todd what's happening?"

He kisses her on the forehead. "I'll tell you tomorrow. For now, go to sleep. I'll be in later."

She nods and walks past him, confused and bewildered, going slowly up the stairs, glancing down a couple times to see if maybe Todd will join her. She does what he said and finds her old earplugs and squashes them into her ears, locking herself inside her head. She is asleep almost before her head hits the pillow.

✷✷✷

Laura opens her eyes and pulls in a shaky, ragged breath. She tugs at the blankets by her knees and yanks herself up until she's sitting. She pants, disoriented and scared. Half recollected images of the night before knock around her brain, disconnected and confusing. She's not sure what is dream and what is memory. Todd is lying on his side of the bed. He's still fully clothed, sleeping above the covers. Even his shoes are still on. As she watches him, she's able to regain control of her breathing and, like a foggy mirror being wiped away, she's able to recall the night before. She thinks about waking Todd, about demanding answers to the series of exceptionally weird events that made up her previous day. His breathing is even and soft, unlike the rusty car engine whine that was usual for him after a night of heavy drinking. She gets the sense that he hasn't been in bed very long. It's something that had never occurred to her before getting married: that she would be able to gauge how long her husband has been sleeping just by looking at him. What odd little gifts marriage gives.

She looks at the clock. 8:23. When Laura was in college, she did a fair amount of drugs. Weed, yes, sometimes MDMA. But she mostly did hallucinogens; she dropped LSD, ate her share of shrooms. She'd wake up the day after one of her trips and spend the first ten or so minutes of wakefulness considering the trip, what she might learn from it, which parts actually happened, which were in her head. The exercise was her favorite part of taking drugs, that feeling of examining a reality that wasn't quite real, the surreal sensation of memory appearing faulty, sometimes glaringly so, as when she watched her college roommate turn into a werewolf before her very eyes.

Laura tries to think of last night through this lens. That everything that happened was a kind of grief-induced

28

hallucination. Her brain was exhausted, unable to grasp the details of her surroundings correctly, and so sending her signals that might tell a story, to explain what she had felt. To explain what she had *thought*.

She considers doing her thinking exercise, but she's tired of thinking about mountains, so she decides to go for a run.

She's not going to think about the previous night. The weight of her missing son is a suit made of sandbags and she knows dwelling on the details of the night before will make the bags swell. She's not sure she can handle the extra weight. She laces up her running shoes and tries to think about nothing.

As she leaves the bedroom, Laura throws one last glance back at her sleeping husband. He looks different. Something about his face. It looks clear, as if he'd been covered in dirt and only just now has cleaned himself. The sight gives her a little flutter in her chest that she doesn't quite recognize.

Her jogging path is usually around the side of the house, past Eddie's bedroom, and down around back. This leads to an opening in the forest marking a path that meanders through the trees and ends at the edge of a dirt road about a mile from their house. Laura steps out the front door and stands on the lawn. She looks at the corner of the house, hiding the way to the path, hiding Eddie's window. Leaning forward and pulling her arm over her head, she does her pre-run stretches. Usually, this takes about three minutes, and then she's off. But today, she lingers in her routine, enjoying the sensation of her muscles waking. She's trying not to think of last night, but she can almost feel that window just out of her view, like it's watching her. The memory of how the sight of that window affected her makes any happy fluttering in her chest cease, like a butterfly splattering against a speeding car windshield. She squeezes her wrist and grits her teeth. She's Laura Sutner. She came in second place at the New England collegiate archery competition when she was at Swarthmore. She ran a hedge fund out of Manhattan for two years before Eddie was born. She raised him, almost by herself, successfully into grade school. Then came Danny, and through it all there were no major errors. Except, of course, for that one really big one. But she doesn't want to think about that right now. She *can't* think about it. She launches herself forward and jogs around the corner.

As expected, there's nothing waiting for her on the other side. It's just a window. There is nothing amiss, no phantom urge to throw the damned thing open. As she passes it, she tries to glance inside to see Eddie, but of course it's more than a foot above her head. She almost goes back inside to check on him, but instead forces herself forward.

The land slopes downhill along the edge of her house, making her steps land uncomfortably hard as she tries to regulate her rhythm. She reaches the bottom of the slope and veers off to the left, the open mouth of the woods greeting her. The opening is canopied; sticks and ivy hang down so that the entrance looks almost deliberate. Somehow the possibility that it isn't unnerves her. The idea that, through the serendipity of nature, a perfectly inviting opening would naturally occur is unexpectedly hideous. As she passes under the proscenium-like canopy, she feels the temperature drop a degree or two, the gloom of the woods taking over. There is still a morning chill in the air and she curses herself for not bringing a windbreaker.

Sunlight pokes through the branches and leaves overhead, making shafts of light like glowing Doric columns. Mourning doves coo dolefully in the high branches, calling to each other about the strange creature running below them. The air is crisp and damp from the morning dew. *The morning dew releases you,* she thinks, as she often does, though she's not sure what the provenance of the phrase is. The woods feel safe to her. The sound of her feet hitting the pine-needled floor of the forest is soothing and the farther she gets from the house, the less the memories of last night cling to her brain. Even thoughts of Danny recede for the time being, no small feat. She takes a mental note to start the habit of morning runs. She wasn't truly aware how badly she needed the refuge.

A strange sound invades Laura's calm. She frowns and cocks her head, slowing her gait to try and capture what she's hearing. She stops altogether once she recognizes the sound. Running water. It sounds like a brook, babbling stupidly somewhere in the trees. But that can't be right. She's been frequenting these woods for almost a decade, and never once has she heard the sound of running water along this path, let alone come across any sort of stream or creek. As this thought balloons, something else catches her attention and she looks up at the treetops. The birds have stopped singing. All that remains is the sound of that impossible brook.

Laura knows that she should go home. She should run back to the house and crawl back into bed with her husband, where she'll still be able to pretend that there isn't something deeply wrong invading her life. Laura Sutner is no fool. She knows that the sound of that brook and that crashing is the sound of disaster coiled and ready to spring. She can feel it in the deepest part of herself, the part that called to her even before she entered Danny's room that morning.

But the sound of the brook, it's rather soothing. It feels like a massage on her brain, like it's scratching some buried itch she didn't even know she had. She can picture it: clear, catching sunlight, alive with movement, polished stones at its bottom. It reminds her of something from her childhood, a lost emotion she'd forgotten about, or grew out of, maybe.

She breaks from the trail, crashing through the underbrush toward the sound of flowing water. The bushes and low plants are thicker than she anticipated. They have grown dense and stubborn, having experienced little to no intervention by human hands for who knows how long. She lifts her legs as high as she can above the bushes, slicing her exposed flesh on sharp twigs and thorns. The branches seem to pull at her, as if trying to throw her backward and onto the trail, but she moves forward, the sound of water getting louder with each labored step.

Finally, she yanks her foot from a particularly gnarled winterberry bush and finds herself in a small clearing. And there it is, just ten feet ahead of her: the brook. About two feet across, stretching out of sight in either direction. Laura stands at the edge of the clearing, her arms hanging at her side, her mouth slightly open.

This is just not possible. How could she have not heard this sound any of the countless times she's walked along that trail? Not fifteen yards away. Her stomach is getting that sideways feeling from the night before, only this time it seems to be turning over in slow motion, like tiny men inside her are using all their strength to tip it over. She doesn't want to, but she walks slowly to the edge of the water and peers in. The water is black. This is her first and most terrifying thought. But as she stares into the inkiness, she realizes that this is not the case. The brook is simply deep. Very deep. So deep, in fact, that the sunlight refracting off the surface doesn't reach the bottom.

Laura watches her own shimmering reflection, her face contorting with the flow of water, distorted into different versions of herself, now a goblin, now a dragon, now a witch. She steps back and looks around the edge of the brook until she finds a sizable stone, picks it up, and drops it into the water. It makes a tiny splash and she watches it sink, down, down deeper into the black. It disappears before it reaches the bottom.

She needs to go home now. This is suddenly so clear that it comes with an almost physical push, and she stumbles a couple steps backward, wanting to be as far away from the water as possible. She is about to turn and climb back over the bushes when something catches her eye across the brook. There, some distance away, where the forest has grown dense and wily, stands a man, looking at her. From this distance, it looks like he isn't wearing a shirt. Immediately, her stomach begins to roil.

Something's wrong. His proportions are *all wrong*.

His head is too small and his arms dangle long at his sides. He's tall, a good two heads taller than Todd. But the more Laura looks at the man, the less certain she is that it's a man at all. She thinks she can see patches of hair along its naked flesh, and there's something about the head. It looks almost lupine, sloping at an odd angle, creating a face almost like a dog. Could . . . is that a snout?

The feeling of her stomach being turned over has now elevated to a dangerous, corrosive sensation that climbs all the way up to her chest. She staggers back until her rear end is pressed against the winterberry bush. It pricks into her skin as her feet try in vain to push her even further back into the underbrush. The man who is not a man isn't moving. The water roars between them as Laura tries to kickstart her mind into action, to move, to get out of these woods, something foul, something foul is staring at her. It has blue eyes.

This realization severs something in her and she turns, launching herself over the bushes, almost doing a breaststroke through the leaves and branches. There's an alarming barking scream, coming over and over in staccato bursts, and she realizes that it's her own panicked shouts. Unsure why, she turns her head, eyes white and wide as she tears through the foliage. The thing has raised one hand by its head and is moving it back and forth.

It's waving at her.

Fresh screams seem to propel her forward and she lands on her side in the middle of the trail. Everything hurts, but she scrambles up, tears suddenly wet on her face, and she runs faster than she's ever run along the trail back toward her home.

The forest proscenium is just ahead and she has the abrupt lunatic certainty that the vines and branches are going to contract until nothing but a tiny pinprick of light will pierce this now hideous, obscene place and she will be stuck in here with that thing *Jesus Christ what was that thing, oh god, it was smiling, it was smiling.*

But she bursts through the entrance, gasping and sobbing. She turns up the slope, past Eddie's window, around the corner and through the front door. She slams it shut and bolts it, her hands slipping several times, they're shaking so badly. Turning, she lets her back hit the door and slides down until she's sitting, her hands over her eyes, deep terrified sobs tumbling out of her. After a moment, she feels a hand on her arm and she recoils with a scream. But it's just Eddie, looking down at her, concern widening his eyes to saucers. She gropes for him; her arms open in a vague plea for embrace. He gets on his knees and she pulls him to her quivering chest.

"Did you see the tall thing, momma?" he whispers. She nods twice, suddenly understanding.

"I'm sorry," she says, her lips next to his ear. "Eddie, I'm so sorry. I'm sorry."

"It's okay, momma," he says, stroking her shoulder, his voice calm. "We're gonna get Danny back. Dad says Grandma knows how."

At this, she lifts her head to look at her son. His face is still pale and frightened, but there's something else in it. Something that makes her heart rate slow and her bubbling sobs ebb away. She sees Todd in his face. He smiles at her; wan, old beyond his years, and turns his head. She follows his gaze to see the actual Todd standing in the entranceway. He is trying to smile. He is failing.

"Mom will be by in a bit," he says. He strides toward her and leans down.

Eddie crawls out of the way as Todd pulls her up and enfolds her tightly.

"It's going to be okay," he says, quiet, just for her. He releases her and she stands there swaying for a moment. "Go hop in the shower. Eddie and I are going to get ready down here."

She looks at him for a moment, her jaw slack, and her mind numb. She nods and walks past him toward the stairs. As she nears the top, she hears him from below:

"Maybe close the shades while you're at it."

She almost starts crying again. Instead, she giggles in the darkened stairwell.

The thing raises one hand and waves at her.

III. A BROTHER MOURNS

TODD CRAWLS OUT of a dream as dark and cold as a hole in the ground. The details are murky, but there's that lingering feeling that comes with every dream he has of his brother. A sick dread, mixed with smothering shame and a dash of despair. Todd doesn't open his eyes yet, and instead listens to his own breathing and the chirping of the birds in the feeder outside. He can relax when he hears the birds. It's an assurance that his family, for the moment, is safe.

The past week has been, in a word, apocalyptic. For the first few days of Danny's absence, Todd was drunk virtually every waking moment. Every morning he lurched out of a nightmare and reached for the bottle of Jack under his bed. It didn't matter what Laura said to him, how much she begged and pleaded. It was the only thing that kept him from collapsing or driving the car off the steep shoulder on Route 5. When he thinks of it now, he's horrified, and knows that he can try for the rest of his life, but he'll never truly make up for abandoning his wife in the most dire moment of their lives together.

The following days were harder than the first. Laura began to hide the liquor, or throw it out, which sent him on hours-long excursions into town to sit at bars and drink. A couple mornings, he woke up in the back of his car with a migraine that felt like his brain was too big for his skull, threatening to crack open between his eyes. Yesterday was the first day since Danny's disappearance that he didn't drink. He has his mother to thank for that.

Todd opens his eyes and rolls over. Sunlight makes Laura's empty corner of the bed glisten like freshly fallen snow and he sits up, rubbing his eyes. He listens for a moment, waiting for the familiar burble of the coffee maker or the clink and scratch of a pan on the stove. But it's quiet downstairs. She must be on an errand, or a run maybe. The thought of her outside the house on her own gives Todd a little jolt of terror, but the sun pouring through the window and the birds singing outside dull the sharp blades of panic. As long as she doesn't linger too long, and stays out of the woods, she should be fine.

He thinks about what his mother told him last night. Everything about his brother. About his father. He always knew, in some primordial part of himself, that this was going to happen. The details, as they were when he was a child, were murky. But that crawling, ever-present dread has been a part of his life for as long as he can remember. And now it has subsumed his life and taken his son away from him.

Though, since yesterday, Todd now has something that he thought was lost forever: a tiny, precious glimmer of hope.

He swings his legs over the side of the bed and is surprised to see his boots are still on his feet. The memory of the previous night suddenly grips him and he stands, wobbly as a spinning top. The flashlight is still on his bedstand and there's dirt in the treads of his boots. After he sent Laura to bed, he had gone to the downstairs closet and pulled out the flashlight. Before he could lose his nerve, he'd stormed out the back door and gone to Eddie's window. There was nothing there, of course. But the woods behind the house seemed darker than they should have been, and the crickets' song was tepid and uncertain, as if they had just started up again after a long silence. Todd stood under his son's window, the woods behind him like an approaching storm. The bottom of the window frame was a good six inches taller than him, and there was a smell lingering in the air. Like rotting fruit in a musty cellar. He pointed the flashlight at the ground. Footprints as long as his forearm led away from the window into the shadowy labyrinth of the forest.

Todd stands and walks to the other side of the room, the floorboards creaking beneath his feet. He picks up the phone and dials the number he knows by heart. The phone rings as he walks to the edge of the bed and sits heavily. Something clinks and clatters to the floor under the bed. He leans down and pulls the half empty bottle of Jack Daniels from under the curtain of sheets and blankets. The brown liquid sloshes behind the glass, warm and inviting. He regards the bottle for a moment, then sets it on the floor between his feet. The receiver clicks, and Sandy's voice fills his ear.

"Todd," she says, all business, as if he's a client and they're commencing an official transaction.

He smiles. "Hi, mom," he says. He hears the clinking of china, then the soft sound of pouring water. He gets the distinct impression that she's been waiting till he called to take her tea.

"Slept off the liquor, I trust?"

Todd winces. When his mother had summoned him yesterday, he had been about five shots deep and it showed. They hadn't even been able to talk properly until Todd took a nap and drank some coffee.

"Uh-huh," he says. Then: "Sorry about that."

Sandy makes a dismissive tsk-ing sound. "It's alright. Believe me, I understand. We're all trying to keep our heads up." Her tone grows sharp. "But no more of that. Do you understand?"

Todd smiles again. He can't help it. "Yeah, mom, I understand."

She makes a satisfied *humph*! sound. "Good. Now. I'm glad you called. I know we left things a little up in the air last night, and I know it was a lot of information to take in all at once. Have you talked to Laura about it?"

"No, not yet."

"Do. As soon as possible. It doesn't make sense for her to be in the dark."

"I agree."

There's a rustling sound on the other end of the line, followed by his mother grunting. He pictures her settling into her favorite armchair, the one by the window overlooking the field out back. As a boy, he and his brother would sit at her feet while she roosted in that chair and read them stories from an enormous leather-bound book with gold stenciling. Strange, thrilling stories about frog kings and white snakes. About enchanted talking fish, and princes being thrown into the sea. Those stories made the outside world seem huge and dangerous and magical. Todd spent most of his childhood peering around trees and gazing into ponds, waiting for the magical creature that would change his life forever.

"And what about Eddie?" His mother asks.

Todd shifts and looks at his bedroom door, though he's not sure why. "What about him?"

"Do you think he's seen him?"

Todd swallows and thinks about the footprints below his son's window. "He hasn't said anything."

"Could he be keeping it from you?"

"I don't know. It's entirely possible, but I haven't seen much of him lately. He spends most of his time in his room." That's not really true. Todd hasn't seen much of his son because he hasn't wanted to. Seeing Eddie's wounded, frightened face makes him sick to his stomach. It makes him feel like a failure.

"Does he seem different?" His mother's voice is quiet.

"Yes . . . " Todd says after a moment, though he can't quite find the words to articulate how Eddie is different.

"Like he's ill? You said he's been sick."

"Yes, but the doctor seems to think it's just a byproduct of . . . of the circumstances we're in . . . "

Sandy makes a scoffing noise and he hears the sound of the armchair creaking as she rises. He imagines her pacing across the rug in her small living room.

"Dr. Amleth, right? The man's a quack, and he doesn't have all the information now, does he? Have you talked to Eddie about it?"

"No, I haven't . . . "

"You should. The situation calls for it."

"Look, if that's the case, then it's a lot more serious than-"

"Of course it's serious, Todd," she cuts him off, impatient. "You know what the endgame is."

"Okay."

"This needs to be dealt with today."

"Yes, okay. But this isn't like last time . . . "

"You don't know that. It could be much worse than last time."

"Yes, but I haven't *seen* anything . . . "

"But you've had the dreams. You continue to have them?"

Todd nudges the bottle with his toe. He's craving a drink, and he's already regretting promising his mother that he wouldn't. "Yes. You do too, right? Like every night? At least since Danny . . . "

"I've dreamt of that wretched creature every night for the past thirty years." Todd pulls the phone away from his ear. Her voice is suddenly filled with a caustic venom that he's not sure he's ever heard from her before. She sighs. "But yes, it's gotten worse since Danny disappeared."

"Well, then maybe you need to talk to him, Mom. After what happened . . . "

"Yes, yes, I'll talk to him. But you have to talk to him first. Tell him what I told you. I'm going to gather some things, and then I'm going to go to Rhonda's to pick up some supplies. You remember Rhonda. With the tall hair? Anyway, she's been hanging onto some little odds and ends for me . . . "

Todd tunes out for a moment. His mother is prone to providing more detail than is strictly necessary, and while he understands that the circumstances are far more dire than usual, he can't help but fall into his old habit of filtering out her words when her speech takes on this particular cadence. Once, when he was in high school, he had a group of friends over for a "game night" (which meant smoking weed in the basement) and his mother, being her enthusiastic self, began regaling his friends with stories of Todd's childhood while she fixed them snacks. As she was known to do, she got lost in her own rambling and let slip that Todd had wet the bed as late as sixth grade. Todd was mortified, and hadn't spoken to his mother for a week after that.

Todd lifts his head. He thinks he heard a floorboard squeak.

". . .I'll need some time to prepare, obviously. This is going to be difficult, to say the least. Eddie needs to be brought up to speed. Laura, too. Talk to your son, Todd."

Todd taps back into Sandy's voice, and nods, forgetting that he's on the phone for a moment. "Okay. Can you come this afternoon? I think he's sleeping now . . . "

"Yes. Like I said, I just need to take some precautions first."

"Should I . . . ?"

"No, you should be fine, as long as you stay indoors."

"Okay. But, Mom, what if—"

"And lock the windows, too."

" . . . Yeah."

"Stay together. We don't want him to isolate any of you. Is Laura there?"

"No. I think she's on a run?"

"Tell her everything I told you when she gets back. You're stronger as a unit, Toddie."

"No, I know, you're right, as usual."

Something moves at the edge of his vision. He looks up to see

Eddie, wide-eyed, peering at him from around the corner of the bedroom door. There's a momentary jolt of surprise, and then he smiles. He motions Eddie over.

"Mom, I have to go. Someone just walked in the room . . . "

"Is it Eddie?"

"Yes. Yes, it is . . . "

His mother sighs, and when she speaks again, her voice is thick with emotion. "Bless that poor brave boy. Tell him his grandma loves him and that everything is going to be okay."

"I will. See you in a few hours . . . "

"Yes. Brace yourself. This is going to be difficult. I love you."

"Love you, too. Bye now."

Todd hangs up and smiles at his son. Eddie looks frightened, but there's also an unmistakable curiosity to his stare. It fills him with a fierce, unexpected love.

He pats the spot next to him on the bed. "Come sit down, Eddie. We have a lot to talk about."

Eddie obeys and climbs onto the bed next to his father.

Todd nudges the bottle back under the bed with his foot and half turns to face his son. "Do you remember your uncle Evan?" Todd asks.

Eddie shrugs. "Not really. Just that he went to jail."

Todd nods, then looks out the window behind his and Laura's bed. He can see the tops of the trees, lined up like an enraptured audience. This is already harder than he expected.

"Do you remember why he went to jail?" Todd asks.

This time, Eddie shows no ambivalence. "He hurt little kids," Eddie says, and there's a change happening on his face. A hardening around the mouth and eyes. He's preparing himself for what Todd is about to say.

"That's right," Todd replies, nodding. "But it's a little more complicated than that."

Eddie pulls himself all the way up onto the bed so he's sitting cross-legged before his father. "Complicated how?" he asks.

Todd folds one leg up onto the bed so he's more fully facing Eddie. He tosses the phone on the comforter and folds his hands. "When I was little, about your age, actually, something bad happened to my dad, your grandpa."

Eddie says nothing; the ever-attentive child.

Todd remembers, for the second time this morning, sitting at his mother's feet, his brother beside him, as she read them strange and wonderful tales. He remembers how desperately he wished they were real. "Dad used to go hunting with his friends in the woods, not far from here. They would hunt deer, mostly, though one time they took down a bear. We had an old bearskin rug for the longest time. Grandma Sandy threw it out eventually. We ate bear for months after that." Todd pulls his other leg up onto the bed, so they mirror each other. "But something happened during one of their trips. Your grandpa got lost in the woods. Later, before things got bad, he said he found a river in the forest and that something came out of the water and . . . and told him things."

Eddie takes a little gulp of air and swallows hard. A part of Todd threatens to crack: he doesn't need to tell Eddie this. He can keep it from him for the rest of his life; Eddie could spend the rest of his days blissfully unaware—maybe even happy. A child shouldn't have to know about this. A child shouldn't be subjected to this horrible reality that's one part fairy tale and two parts unspeakable tragedy. But Todd can't lie to himself. Not anymore. The less Eddie knows, the more danger he's in.

"After that trip, grandpa started to act strangely. He would sleep all day and he talked to us less and less. I remember whenever he looked at me, he would get this look on his face. I . . . I can't describe it really. But it scared me." Actually, Todd knows exactly what the look was. It was hunger; he sees that face almost every night as he sleeps. "After a while, grandpa started to look really sick. Grandma Sandy got really worried and tried to take him to the hospital, but he wouldn't do it and he got really mean. He screamed at her like he never had before. He threw things at her, and me. Evan, too. Grandma didn't try to make him go after that.

"I saw less and less of him over the next few weeks, but every time I did, he seemed taller, more . . . stretched out. And he had started to grow hair in strange places. Like on his arms, his shoulders, his stomach."

Eddie sits up a little straighter and his mouth opens in an unmistakable look of recognition. So that's it then. Eddie's seen him.

"He started to lock himself and Evan in a room and they would talk for hours and hours. Grandma would bang on the door and demand that they come out. But grandpa wouldn't listen. I tried to ask your uncle Evan what they talked about, but he said grandpa made him promise not to. After a while, he wouldn't talk to me at all." The words feel strange in his mouth. He hasn't talked about Evan for years. It's like tasting something foul from your childhood—a long forgotten and sour medicine. "Then, one day, grandpa just . . . disappeared. And I was kind of relieved, if I'm being honest. Grandpa was really scary, and things got better after he left.

"Fast forward fifteen years. I'm living in New York, I had just met your mom, things were going well. We had jobs we liked, you were on the way." Todd flashes a smile at his son and is rewarded with a smaller one from Eddie. A little echo. "Then, out of nowhere, Evan shows up on my doorstep. I just turned the corner and there he was." Todd pauses for a second, remembering. It was a frigid day in January and Todd had been coming home from the post office. He remembers this distinctly because Todd was mailing a letter to his mother, and he had mentioned Evan in passing. He was worried about him; they hadn't spoken in close to a year. So, when Todd discovered his brother, thin as a dying sapling in a pitiful tattered windbreaker on his front stoop, it was as if he had summoned him out of the ether. Like Evan had been waiting for Todd to invoke him.

"He told me he was in trouble and asked if we could talk. I told him okay and we went upstairs. Now, Eddie . . . " Todd leans forward and fixes his son with his most serious, adult stare. Eddie, for his part, is alert to the point of fixation, unblinking beneath his father's intense gaze. "This next part is very hard for me to talk about. I wish I didn't have to tell you, but you need to know how much danger we're in, okay? But we can go slow if you need me to. I'll stop and give you a break if it gets too scary. Okay, kiddo?"

Eddie nods once, almost business-like, a tiny lawyer accepting the terms of an agreement. "I can take it, dad," he says, and Todd's heart lurches with desperate affection and pride.

He exhales. "Uncle Evan told me that, since we were kids, grandpa would make him do things. He said after the hunting trip, grandpa was hungry. Hungry all the time. But he couldn't eat normal food anymore. He could only eat people. Kids." Again, Todd pauses, waiting for his son's reaction. But Eddie doesn't recoil, doesn't gasp. Instead, an expression crosses his face, adult beyond his years, and Todd understands that he's watching the last of his son's innocence shrivel up and die right before his eyes. He allows himself a few heartbeats to mourn before continuing. "Grandpa made him find kids and bring them to him to eat. He said he didn't want to do it, but somehow grandpa could make him do things, just by thinking it. Evan said he'd brought dozens, maybe even hundreds of kids to the woods for grandpa to eat." Todd shakes his head. "But I didn't believe your uncle. I thought it was a horrible, mean joke. Even though—and Eddie, you should know that this is a thing that grown-ups do all the time . . . someday you'll learn to do it too—I knew I was lying to myself. I knew he was telling the truth way deep down at the back of my brain. But I didn't want to believe it. And so I sent uncle Evan away, even though he just needed someone to help him. He just needed his brother." On this last word, Todd's voice breaks for the first time. He puts a hand over his eyes, determined to retain his composure. Crumbling now would destroy the delicate emotional balance that he's achieved with his son. He takes a few deep breaths and when he pulls his hand away, he sees that Eddie's eyes are shining.

"It wasn't until last year that I saw my brother again. This time, it was in court. And I'm sure you remember that."

Eddie nods and manages to keep his waiting tears at bay.

"I had convinced myself that uncle Evan was lying. To me, to himself. So he could feel better about hurting all those kids. But that was stupid. I lied to myself. And now your brother is missing." Todd looks out at the trees again. The wind has picked up and the branches jitter anxiously in the breeze—a line of sentinels, raising the alarm. "You've seen your grandpa, haven't you, Eddie?"

"Yeah," Eddie says. His voice is husky.

An unpleasant shot of electricity shoots through Todd. He tries to stop himself from asking the question on the tip of his tongue. He fails. "How did he look?"

"Bad. Really bad," Eddie says, almost a whisper.

"Can you describe him?"

Eddie shifts, then looks away for the first time. Todd wants to tell him nevermind, don't bother. You don't have to relive that, kiddo. But he doesn't.

"He . . . it was like he was all droopy. And his fur was almost gone." Fur. Not hair. The distinction makes Todd's stomach churn. "He just looked really sick and thin. He told me to open the window and he would take me to Danny. But I didn't do it, even though I kinda wanted to, except I didn't *really* want to. It was like someone was telling me to do it, but from right here." He points to the spot between his eyes. "I didn't do it, Dad. I knew he was lying."

Todd smiles and pulls Eddie into a one-armed hug. Eddie leans against his shoulder.

"You did so good, bud. That must have been so scary."

"It was really *really* scary," Eddie says, his voice muffled against Todd's shirt. Now Eddie does cry, just a little. A few quiet, tired sobs.

Todd thinks it's more from relief than anything else. Confirmation from an adult that he's not just telling scary stories.

Eddie pulls away and wipes his tears. "Is Danny dead?" he asks. He's the frightened child again, unprepared and unable to fully accept or even consider the idea, but asking because he can't help himself.

A wave of hatred for his own father roars through Todd; if he gets the chance, he will tear apart the creature that used to be his father until there's nothing but gristle and bone. And then he'll burn what's left.

"I don't know," Todd says truthfully. "I really don't, Eddie, and I'm sorry that I can't tell you for sure. But Grandma Sandy thinks he might still be alive."

"Really?" Eddie asks. The little spark of hope that lights up his eyes almost makes Todd regret saying this. But they're in it now. Half-truths and ambivalence would be a mistake.

"Have you ever heard someone say 'better to have a fishing rod than a fish?'" Todd asks. Eddie cocks his head, then shakes it. Todd grips his son's shoulder and once again fixes him with his most adult *I'm-trusting-you-with-this* stare. "Grandma thinks he's trying to do to you what he did to your uncle Evan. She thinks he's going to try to train you to bring him other kids. She thinks Danny might be alive so that . . . do you know what leverage is? Doesn't matter. The point is Danny might be alive so he can use your brother as bait. To reel you in." Eddie gazes at his father, his fear and anxiety now cut through with wonder.

"What are we gonna do, Dad?" he asks.

Todd tightens his grip on his son's shoulder, and he's reminded, vividly, of last winter, watching Eddie carry a snow-suited Danny through the deep, fluffy snow. The big brother. Proud and watchful. "If you say it's okay," Todd says, "we're going to let him."

Downstairs, the door slams, hard. A moment later, they hear Laura's terrified, wailing voice, drifting up the stairs like a ghost made of fire. They exchange a look of surprise, and then Eddie is off the bed and tearing down the stairs. Todd lingers for a moment. He takes a shuddery breath, then follows his son downstairs to fix what has been broken.

✲

The light has gone a soft butter yellow and afternoon shadows crawl like spiders across the living room floor. Todd's family huddles together, Laura on the couch between himself and Eddie—curled up against her like a protective puppy; and Sandy, stout, stern, and alert on the blue armchair across the coffee table. Laura has recounted her story three times. With each iteration, she becomes a little clearer, a little more in control, until she's able to repeat the story to Todd's mother without collapsing into violent shaking.

"How deep was the water?" Grandma Sandy asks.

Laura shakes her head. "I don't know. The rock disappeared before it hit the bottom. Too deep." She says this last bit to Todd, who shakes his head in return.

There has never been water of any sort in those woods. He knows that for a fact.

Sandy leans back and sighs so deeply she seems to lose three inches. "The hour is late," she intones, like she's a character in one of her fairy tales: the sage old magician swooping in to save the children in peril. But his mother doesn't look like the stolid, dependable characters illustrated in her gold-stenciled tome. She looks like a frightened old lady, given the impossible task of saving her family from a ravenous, mad monster. As fragile and human as Todd has ever seen her. "He's getting desperate. I don't think he would have shown himself to you if he wasn't. If Danny is alive, we likely don't have much time before he . . . before he succumbs to his urges." The implication hangs like a poisonous cloud over the room and Eddie curls tighter against Laura.

Todd's mother shifts in her seat and looks out the window. "He's become something unpredictable, more animal than human. But if there's any of him left in there, I think there's a chance for Danny." She turns to look at Eddie, diminished by fear and exhaustion so that he looks closer to the child Todd remembers when he first learned to walk in this very room. Completely unprepared for what the adults are asking of him. "Eddie," Sandy says, leaning forward.

Eddie unfurls himself and sits, giving his grandma his full attention.

"Do you understand the plan?"

Eddie nods.

"Do you feel like you're up to it?"

Eddie looks to his parents. For permission? For rescue? Todd can't tell, and is on the verge of calling it off when Laura speaks.

"We can't make him do this, mom," she says, grabbing Eddie's hands with both of hers. Her tremor has returned, and Todd puts an arm around her so his family forms a protective daisy chain around his son. "This is way too much. What if something goes wrong? What if he takes Eddie, too?" Todd's mother offers a tired smile, and she reaches across the table to put a hand on both of Laura's, completing the connection.

"I don't like it either. You're right, it's too much to ask of him. And he's been so brave already. If Eddie doesn't want to do it, we'll think of something else." She pulls her hand away and looks again at Eddie. "But I think it *should* be Eddie's decision. None of us have been able to fix this. I think you deserve the option, at least." She says the last bit just for him, a private communication between grandmother and grandson.

Eddie pulls his hand away and pinches his eyes between thumb and forefinger, a distinctly grown-up gesture. His son seems to be caught in some sort of aging purgatory, vacillating between frightened child and beleaguered adult at the drop of a hat.

"I want to try," he says to Laura, who shakes her head, makes a small sound of despair. "If it means we might get Danny back . . . I want to try."

Grandma Sandy grunts, her familiar sound of satisfaction. "It's settled then. At dusk, the three of us will take the car and leave Eddie here. We'll park just around the corner." Sandy points out the window to the dirt road that curves around a copse of trees and out of sight. "Your dad will come back and watch you from the woods, just in case. If I'm not mistaken, he'll lead you to your brother, Eddie, and we'll follow with this." She reaches into the bag beside her chair and pulls out a small caliber revolver. It glints in the dying sun. "I've been preparing for this day. The bullets in this gun are silver and coated in lamb's blood. Not easy to come by, I'll tell you what. But from what I've been able to figure out, it should do the trick."

Eddie eyes the gun with the appropriate awe and terror, but the sight of it fills Todd with a sick, almost prophetic dread. He reaches for the gun and his mother hands it to him, their eyes connecting for a fleeting, meaningful moment. He stows it in his pocket, sure to check the safety before he does.

"This is insane," says Laura. "We can't actually be doing this. Can't we just search the woods again? I found him once."

Grandma Sandy shakes her head. "You'll only see him if he wants you to see him. The police would have found them already if they were in plain sight. He's hiding. He's good at hiding." She says this with an air of long-nurtured anger, anger that's curdled into a ripe hatred. Todd can identify. "We move at dusk," she says again. "And by this time tomorrow, Danny will be safe in his crib, god willing."

The four of them lapse into silence, listening to the wind pester the trees and waiting for the sun to slink away and throw their troubled home into shadow.

✳✳✳

The wind is picking up. Todd had always wanted a house at the forest's edge. He liked the feeling of enclosure, the sense—erroneous as it turned out to be—of having a barrier between his family and the rest of the world. But now, the way the wind tugs at the trees, making them scream in protest . . . it's making him antsy. He's worried that all the movement and sound between them could easily obscure something lurking in the gloom. Shapes appear, then skitter into nothing, only to return more sharply: a grasping hand, a hungry face. Teeth.

Todd stands with his son at the edge of the porch while his wife and mother pile into the car in the driveway below. Eddie is pale, but he looks determined. Todd is struck by how sturdy the kid turned out to be; braver than his father by a mile. While Todd nearly drank himself to death, Eddie was facing down monsters and protecting the house from incursion. Had things gone a different way, Eddie could have been his grandfather's second victim, and that, likely as not, would have been it for Todd.

He would have abandoned Laura permanently, launching himself off that steep shoulder on route 5. The thought fills him with shame, but Todd seems to have lost the ability to lie to himself. He's a coward. His son is made of far stouter stuff than he. And for that, at least, Todd is grateful.

He squeezes Eddie's shoulder and his son jumps, washing away the image of the brave soldier going off to war. He's just a kid. And Todd's about to feed him to the wolves.

"Last chance to change your mind, kiddo," Todd says, quiet. It's almost lost to the wind. "No one will be mad if you do."

Eddie shakes his head. "I'm his brother," he says simply. "It's what big brothers do, right? They protect their little brothers?"

Todd studies him, but there's no hint of accusation or anger in his face. It's the lesson he's taking from this whole mess, Todd sees that clear as day. He wants to pick his son up, squeeze him, tell him none of this is his responsibility. This is not supposed to be his to fix.

Instead, he pulls him into a side hug. Eddie leans against him and they stare into the forest.

"You're the bravest person I know, Eddie," Todd says.

"I don't feel brave," Eddie whispers.

Todd barely catches it over the howling in his ears. "That's what being brave is. Doing something even if you're scared." Eddie doesn't respond to this as the wind tumbles hard over the treetops, scattering dead leaves like confetti. Todd lingers, wanting to savor these last few moments with his son.

"Todd," Sandy calls from below.

He looks down to see her standing by the car. She beckons to him.

Todd squeezes Eddie once more, then turns and walks down the porch steps to the passenger door before he can stop himself. He slides in and his mom gets in the back. Laura turns on the car and pulls out of the driveway. Todd watches Eddie, standing lonely atop the porch steps. Eddie stares back and raises his hand in a small wave. He tries to smile. He fails. Todd watches him until the car pulls around the corner and his son and home are lost to impeding trunks and branches.

Laura drives a few hundred yards, then neatly pulls the car into a U-turn and stops so the house is just out of sight. She turns off the car. The three of them sit as the engine cools and the wind moans.

"I don't like this," Laura says quietly. "This is a supremely bad idea."

"I don't disagree with you," Sandy says from the backseat.

Todd hears her unbuckle her seatbelt and slide to the middle seat, but doesn't see her. He's straining to peer through the trees to see his son, but the forest hides him.

"Do you remember . . . " Laura starts, turning to Todd. He tears his gaze from the trees to look at her. She's just as pale as Eddie was. " . . . when Eddie was two and he hit his head on the coffee table?"

He nods. "Yeah. Blood everywhere. Three stitches. What a nightmare."

Laura squeezes her wrist and sets her jaw. "I would give anything to go back to that. I thought that was the scariest thing that would ever happen to him." She shakes her head, helpless. "This is wrong, Todd."

"I know," he says, and turns back to stare through the crowded forest. "I think we might be bad parents."

Shadows sprawl as they wait, blending together until the last copper dregs of light fizzle in the sky behind them. All around the car, leaves drift to the ground and are caught in sudden gusts before being borne away, deeper into the forest where they'll land, rot, and become a part of the soil. The temperature drops and Todd's heart grows cold. He believes, all at once, that Laura is right. They've made a terrible error.

"Graaaandpaaaaaaa!" Eddie's voice, high and tremulous, glides to them on a rush of wind.

Laura's breath catches.

"It's time," Sandy says.

Without another word, Todd opens the car door and steps into the cold November air.

The wind rises, and the trees cackle and clatter in the meager light. Twilight is alive with jostling, grasping arms and bodies, elbowing each other out of the way to get a better look at the man who's sacrificed his son to the night. Todd looks over his shoulder into the windshield, but it's too dark: he can't even see his wife's silhouette, though he can feel her gaze through the glass. He can almost hear her pulsing, singular thought: *Fix this.* Turning back to the trees, he wraps his hand around the revolver's grip and crosses the barrier between road and forest.

The wind may actually be of use to him. The snapping of twigs and branches beneath his feet is masked by the incessant howl of the wind and the trees' returning rattle. Were the night still and quiet, he could be heard coming from a mile away. As he maneuvers around clawing branches and over rotting logs, however, he understands the inverse to be true as well: he will not be able to hear his father's approach.

"Graaaaaaaaandpaaaaaaaaaa!" Eddie calls again, and his voice sends an unpleasant shiver down Todd's spine. The house is ahead; he can see slivers of the porch light shining between the trees like shards of a broken mirror. Why did they only leave him that one light? What were they thinking?

Finally, he reaches the other side of the copse of trees and crouches behind a trunk by the edge of the road. The house is a slumbering beast, its mouth hanging open, gulping in the shuddering night air like water. Eddie stands, a shadow in the porch light; a small, lost silhouette, poised in the mouth of a behemoth, soon to be swallowed. Todd's grip on the revolver tightens.

Eddie cups his hands to his mouth.

"Graaaaaaaaaandpaaaaaaaaa!" His voice is a piercing note that mingles into uneasy harmony with the wind—two voices, beckoning. The remaining light of day has retreated and nothing remains but ambiguous, lurching shadows; any moment now, one will free itself from the rest and come to claim his son.

Todd scans the edges of what is ostensibly his property, but has, sometime between abandoning Eddie on the porch and now, turned to an alien landscape over which he has no true control. It strikes him as protean, ancient. A land much older than man, a place where only primordial, vicious creatures hold dominion and skulk about, guided by their propulsive hunger. Todd shivers and wishes he brought a jacket.

The night howls, and Todd waits. Above, dark clouds glide across the moonless sky, hiding, then revealing stars. He imagines them as boats on a river, their inhabitants peering down upon the performance below, only passingly intrigued before moving on to haunt another corner of the sky. It's in this moment, or collection of moments, that Todd feels more alone than he has ever felt. He looks to his son, standing lonely across a vast sea of darkness, and understands how forsaken he must feel. How horribly, terribly forgotten.

"Graaaaaaaaaaaand-!" Eddie's voice cuts off mid-call. The shadow that is his son takes a step backward, then another.

Todd's body vibrates with fresh adrenaline and he scans the environs once more, searching for isolated movement amongst the crowd of nature.

At the forest edge, near the top of the driveway, a shadow detaches itself from the monolith of dark. It stands tall, more than a foot taller than Todd, but instead of walking toward the porch, it drops to all fours, and begins to scrabble like vermin across Todd's lawn. His skin crawls as he watches its progress. The thing's movements are unnatural, hitching like broken gears, spasmodic and unintuitive. Watching it as it jerks its way toward Eddie, Todd understands that the thing that was his father is deeply, deeply sick. Starving, yes; nearing the end of its life, yes. But there's something in Todd's base DNA that tells him that beneath these banal, organic maladies, there is a pestilence in the very soul of this creature that defies nature itself. It is not of the natural order, he realizes, and he is overcome by the horrible recognition of the shadow behind the creeping shadow. Todd looks instinctively to the heavens, with half a certainty that he will see the abomination's maker glowering down from above.

On the porch, Eddie staggers backward, hits the open screen door. Todd hears it clatter over the cackling of the forest. *Steady, kiddo,* Todd thinks to himself. *Be brave for your brother.* The creature slows. There's a moment of suspension, instincts passing between Eddie and his grandfather, leaping over Todd's own generation like a child over a brook. Then, Eddie turns and runs back into the house, as the screen door—but not the oak front door—slams shut behind him. Todd almost screams.

"No," he whispers. "No, no, no, no, no." Eddie wasn't supposed to go inside. Inside, he'll be trapped. Todd won't be able to follow them to Danny. The plan hinges on Eddie allowing his grandfather to lead him into the forest. He silently wills Eddie to reappear, to open the door and face down the monster. But the door stays shut.

The thing reaches the steps and rises. Beneath the harsh porch light glare, the figure of the creature becomes defined. Details are lost, but Todd is reminded with hideous clarity of the last time he saw his father. It lurches like a worm up the steps, his earliest nightmare made flesh: the head is too small, and its proportions are wrong, suggesting something more lupine than human; its arms hang long at its sides, and its legs stretch like broken spindles; tufts of hair twitch and shimmer in the wind, islands in the pink, sagging flesh. It walks without hurry to the screen door. It hooks a long finger in the door handle, then sends a sharp, calculated glance over its shoulder. Todd's chest tightens. Does it see him? Has it sensed him on the wind? Before he can decide if it has, the creature opens the door and vanishes into the gullet of Todd's home.

Todd curses, waits for a moment, then moves from his cover and across the lawn, his body low to the ground, the gun held too tightly in his trembling grip. He reaches the porch steps and climbs them soundlessly. In this sole pocket of light, Todd feels too exposed; he peers through the screen door into his darkened home, straining to see inside. But the curtain of porch light hides the interior. Todd opens the door, praying that it doesn't squeal, and tiptoes over the threshold after his father.

The dark is absolute. Todd remains motionless on his haunches, waiting for his eyes to adjust. Slowly, objects swim out of the dark like fish to the surface of a pond. The familiar details of his home—the hall table with the large fruit bowl on top; the grandfather clock ticking at the end of the hall; the doorways to the kitchen, living room, and bathroom looming like worried figures in the dark; and the stairway that leads up to his and Laura's bedroom. Todd listens. Deeper in the house: the scrape of a foot against wood; labored breathing. Todd moves silently across the runner that his mother gave them as a moving-in present and down the hall, toward Laura's study and Eddie's bedroom.

He stops at the corner and tilts his head just enough to see the outline of Laura's study door, parallel to him, closed tight, and the yawning mouth of Eddie's room gaping at the end of the hallway. Something large shifts, dark against dark, and Todd sees the outline of the thing duck its head and enter Eddie's room. Todd double checks that the gun is cocked, then moves down the hall an inch at a time, trying to remember where each floorboard will creak beneath his weight.

"There you are," it whispers. The sound of it skitters out of the gloom like an insect and Todd freezes, his hair standing on end. The voice is clotted with age and disease, but there is no mistaking it: it is his father's voice, calling to him from the nightmare of his childhood. "Come out of there, Eddie," the thing croaks. "Let me see you."

Todd reaches Eddie's bedroom and stops. Eddie is standing with his back pressed to the window. Todd can just see the whites of his wide, horrified eyes staring at the hulking figure in the dark.

"Good boy, Eddie, that's my good boy," the thing croons and takes a step closer. A wave of stink wafts off its body and Todd has to clap a silent hand to his nose and mouth, eyes watering. It smells like a rotting animal, cut through with a sour note of spoiled milk. Something else, too. Something floral, almost fruity. Todd suppresses a gag.

"Don't touch me," Eddie wheezes, and the screen in the window crinkles as he tries to push himself even further back. "Don't touch me, please." The thing stops its tepid progress. Its breathing is getting faster.

"I won't hurt you, Eddie," it says, and reaches out as if to stroke him. Eddie moans and it pulls its hand back, uncertain—a distinctly human gesture. It makes Todd nauseous. "I need your help, Eddie. Grandpa needs your help."

"W-will you bring me to Danny?" Eddie asks, his voice shaky, close to tears. He's making tiny, high-pitched moaning noises every few seconds: the sound of a trapped animal.

"Yesssss," it hisses, and takes a step closer to Eddie. This time it doesn't recoil when Eddie whimpers. It's growing bolder. "Take my hand," it says, and Todd sees long fingers extend in the dark. Todd aims, ready to shoot.

The grandfather clock bellows behind him and Todd flinches so hard he almost loses his balance. Eddie and his father lurch, too, and Todd knows what's going to happen a fraction of a second before it does.

His father whips his head toward the door in search of the noise's source and their eyes lock from across the room. Even in the poor light, Todd recognizes them: electric blue. They widen with recognition. Eddie manages a soft "no . . . !" But the gears are already in motion.

The creature's whole form becomes taut; a coiled energy that reminds Todd of a snake. Todd has time to look at Eddie, to see the sick, resigned horror on his face. Todd makes it two steps toward him before his father lets out an ear-piercing shriek like knives on metal, and it's bounding across the room toward Eddie, a loping, ancient beast. He scoops Eddie up like he weighs nothing—over the sudden cacophony, Todd hears him make a small sound; a tiny "oh!" of surprise—and together they crash through the bedroom window, the glass exploding outward into the screaming night.

IV. I SAW IT COMING, I LET IT BE

THIS WAS NOT the life Sandy had envisioned for herself. When she was a young mother, right after Todd was born, she had been in love with the notion of a simple, quiet life; a life spent supporting her husband and boys, content to watch her family bloom like a well-tended garden. Her parents had taught her—in more ways than one—that the greatest goal she could possibly achieve was to be a caring, resilient wife and mother. That she need only depend on the men she loved to shape a life full of joy and free of sorrow. Boy, what a crock of shit that turned out to be.

Every man in her life, she muses, sitting in the back seat of her son's car, staring through the darkening windshield, has failed her. Her husband turned out to be a monster worthy of nothing but a swift death; her youngest had followed him blindly into depravity and ruin. And, though she hates to admit it, Todd is his own sort of failure: despite her consistent warnings since Eddie's birth, he had lied to his wife, systematically, over many years, then allowed her grandson to be stolen. Her idea of a good life had collapsed around her, all of it in excruciating slow motion.

She had long abandoned this dream of an easy family life, and had been surprised to find—with an occasional flash of shame—that her new, more solitary existence had suited her much better. It wasn't until all the men had slunk away to their separate corners that she began to really know herself. And she had found, to her great delight, that she was excellent company.

"Graaaaaandpaaaaaaaaa!" Eddie's voice comes drifting into the car from another world. Sandy leans forward on her aching knees and sighs through her nose. In the front seat, Laura shifts, clearly antsy. Outside, the wind has taken on a manic, agitated quality that

Sandy doesn't much care for. Through all her years of private study, she had gleaned a great deal about the natural world and how humans—and other, viler things—communed and interacted with it. Ideas of interconnectivity, of all nature being in conversation with itself, permeated the works she perused. There is also the idea—ridiculous, in Sandy's opinion—that nature despises that which is outside its natural order, and will react accordingly: this being the rationale for freak disasters from some of the kookier corners of the internet. It's preposterous to think that the trees know that there's a monster in their midst, that the wind can smell an abomination. But still. The way the branches wave at her, like they're trying to get her attention, trying to warn her . . . it seems more plausible now than it did in the daylight.

"Graaaaaandapaaaaaaaa!" Eddie's voice comes again. Laura grips the steering wheel and rests her forehead on top.

"This was a mistake," she mumbles into the car horn. "I can feel it in my stomach."

Sandy doesn't reply. There's a growing worry in her own gut that Laura may be right: Sandy may have gravely miscalculated.

Perhaps there is none of her husband left. Perhaps the impulse that guided him to groom Evan instead of devour him has been obliterated by the new thing he's become. Perhaps Danny is now no more than a pile of tiny bones somewhere in the forest, soon to be joined by Eddie's.

"How did this happen?" Laura asks. She lifts her head to look at Sandy, as if expecting an answer.

Sandy blinks at her, surprised. "How do you mean?" she asks.

Laura gestures to the windshield, to the events transpiring somewhere out there in the dark, beyond where the last bit of sunlight can reach. "All of this," she says, sounding impatient, like she's angry that Sandy can't track her thoughts. "None of it makes any sense to me."

Sandy gazes out the windshield. Their field of vision is shrinking rapidly, the curve of the road dwindling away, so that all she can make out are the trees in their immediate vicinity, like they're being slowly surrounded by a herd of strange, looming animals.

"It doesn't make any sense to me either, Laura," Sandy says quietly. "I've scoured the internet, ticked off more than a few librarians, and it's still murky." Now she looks to Laura and sees an echo of her former self: the distraught mother, driven nearly to madness by the surreal horror that has consumed her life. "I wish I had answers to give, I do. But if there are answers, they're not accessible to me. And part of me feels that I don't want to know what's truly happening. I'm not sure our brains are built to know."

Laura turns back to the windshield. Their line of sight has shrunk even further, and her face is not much more than a rough outline. "I keep thinking about the water," she says. "It's like it's stuck up here." She points to the side of her head.

Sandy nods, though Laura is facing away from her. She, too, is most troubled by the water. The rest she can place somewhere—however clumsily—within her understanding of physics and nature; grasping explanations that, if she squints hard enough, can account for the horrible events of her life. But the water. The reason for that eludes her.

"When he came back from the hunt, before he was all the way gone, he talked about it. The water," Sandy says.

Laura turns slowly, as if processing the information. She gives Sandy a look—a look that says she doesn't want to hear this, but cannot turn the information away.

"What did he say?" she asks. The trees press closer, leaning in to hear.

"A great deal," Sandy says. "Before he started to change, it was all he could talk about. He said he was in the deer stand, alone, when he heard running water. It was strange, of course. To suddenly hear the sound of water where there was none before . . . a very peculiar feeling." She fixes Laura with a look, wanting to see her reaction. But her face is inscrutable, and difficult to see in the fog of encroaching night. "He followed the sound and there it was, just a few hundred yards away. A stream, only a few feet across, babbling away like it had been there all along. But when he looked in . . . the water was deep. 'Ocean deep,' I remember him saying. He always looked so far away when he said it. *Ocean deep.*" Sandy shakes her head as a chill runs through her. Night has fully arrived; it pushes against the car, prying its way in. "Then, he said, something came from below the surface. He watched it rise to meet him." Sandy pauses as a gust of wind rocks the car, making it squeal on its shocks. *Speak not of it,* a voice calls from deep in her head. Somewhere in the night, Eddie calls for his grandfather.

"What did he see?" the shadow in the front seat whispers.

"I . . . he could never really say. Sometimes he said there was a light, sometimes a face, a woman's face. He once woke up screaming about eyes. And teeth. How he was being eaten. 'I can feel it biting me, Sandy,' he said. He showed me his chest, where he said he could feel its bite. But I didn't see anything." She can't see Laura's face at all anymore. "Did *you* see anything, Laura?" Sandy asks.

The shadow shakes its head no. "Only water," Laura replies. Her voice is strange, slow and quiet, like she's drowsy. The wind howls in protest.

"I think we should stop talking about it," Sandy says abruptly.

Laura's shadow nods. It looks as if it takes great effort. "Yes," she says. "It . . . makes me . . . feel strange."

"Graaaaaaan—!" Eddie's voice snaps off, clean as a dry branch. Whatever spell cast over the car breaks too and Laura reels back, gasping. Sandy could be imagining it, but she thinks she feels a strange electricity in the air. A storm of pollution.

"He's here," Sandy says.

"Oh, god," Laura whispers.

Sandy strains to hear any sound beyond the howling of the wind. The plan feels creakier and creakier the more she considers it. They should have done it in the daylight. They should have devised a signal. They shouldn't have sent Todd alone to follow them into the forest. A thought occurs to Sandy; a thought that brings with it the cold, terrible ring of truth: perhaps the plan was not hers at all.

The thought makes her feel, for the first time in many years, instinctually frightened, the way one would feel in the presence of a powerful, lurking predator. She hugs her arms to keep herself from bolting out in the night.

The minutes bloat and decay, and Sandy is reminded of the last time she had to wait for monsters to decide her fate. A couple months after her husband's return from his hunting trip, he had vanished into the woods behind their house. At this point, he had started to grow hair, his body stretching like taffy, his speech monosyllabic. She had watched him from the kitchen window as he lumbered through the backyard and was swallowed by the trees. Even then she knew that if she ever saw him again, it wouldn't be for many many years. A lifetime.

But still, she waited. She sat by the window, clinging with desperate hope to that life she had dreamt of. He would come back out of the forest, cured, her husband returned to her, ready to take up the mantle of father and caregiver once more. It was a fantasy, she knew. A silly story. And as the night began to claw its way out from behind trunks and branches, Sandy had stood, resolved to drag him back to reality with her own two hands.

Out of the black, the rapturous shattering of glass; the air quivers and Sandy feels the fragile framework of their plan bend, then splinter along with it. Laura screams, a sound that is not quite human, and before Sandy can form a coherent thought, Laura opens the car door and vanishes into the dark.

For the second time in her life, Sandy's world is collapsing. But this time, it's happening much, much faster. She can feel it slipping away, dissolving to dust, and as she tears the car door open and follows a screaming Laura into the night—alive with the cacophonous wailing of the wind and the stampede of panicking trees—she feels the resigned, sickening epiphany curdle in her gut: she knew this was going to happening. *I saw it coming*, she thinks as she catches Laura's shadow slip into the trees, toward the shimmering shards of light that is her home. *I saw it coming, I let it be.*

"DAAADDDDDYYYYY!" Eddie's scream is a dagger through her skull; she stumbles as if struck, and when she rights herself, her breath tumbles out of her in little screaming gasps. Her knees threaten to buckle and her lungs are already a flaming coal bellows. As the light from the house grows clearer, the hope within her flickers, goes out.

What Sandy sees in the next few moments will hover at the forefront of her memory for the rest of her days—a painting hung in the foyer of her mind that, try as she might, she'll never be able to remove.

The light in Eddie's room has been turned on, casting sickly, yellow light onto the lawn like the gaze of some cosmic, fiendish beholder. At the edge of the house, coming around from the porch, Todd's shadow charges toward the light like a suicidal moth to flame. Ahead of her, Laura stagger-runs to her son, screaming his name with every step, arm outstretched as if she can cease the horror transpiring before her.

In the pool of revealing light, her husband stands, bent over a small figure writhing in his grip. The creature's mouth is open; teeth glimmer like the glass on the ground around them—a second mouth, poised to devour. Laura screams, Todd sprints, Eddie struggles. The beast leans in to close its jaw around Eddie's neck. Compelled by something beyond her understanding, Sandy stops and plants herself. She inhales the wind.

"*WILLIAM!!*" Sandy bellows with the force of nature itself. The wind rushes around her, carrying her voice like a boat on a wave, amplifying it, filling it with the authority of the soil, the trees, the sky.

For a few heartbeats, all is frozen. Even the wind slinks away and the trees quiet. From across the lawn, glittering with glass, she sees the creature lift its deformed head. It looks to her, and though it should be impossible in the paltry light, she sees his electric blue eyes—startled into recognition.

William returns. For a scant, shimmering moment, the beast retreats and her husband is staring at her with a question on his face. *Sandy?* His expression seems to ask. *What's happening to me?*

Then Eddie's hand shoots out and slaps the creature's glistening chest, trying to pry himself from its grip, and the spell is broken. Its face contorts into that of a frightened, angry animal. A flash of bloodied skin and fur, and the monster barrels into the forest, Eddie struggling in his arms, the dark drinking them up like ink dropped in ink.

Todd takes off as Laura shrieks after the vanishing shadow. He follows his father into the shadows, screaming Eddie's name.

"Todd, get him!" Laura pleads. She's running toward the place where Todd has vanished.

"Wait, Laura, don't-!" But it's too late. Before Sandy can move another step, her entire family has melted into the forest, leaving her nothing but the wind for company.

Sandy called her husband's name and received no answer.

The forest was gloomy and strangely unfamiliar. Her family had walked these trails together countless times, and though her feet carried her without issue along the darkened path, she found that everything looked off-kilter, like an artist's rendering of the woods behind her house.

"Wiiiiiilllliiiiiaaaaam!" she called, cupping a hand to her mouth. Somewhere in the treetops, a crow called back, mourning the coming night.

Decades later, as Sandy barrels through another forest miles away, she is seized by a certainty that she has been transported through time, back to the days when her boys were still boys and the full horror of her life had yet to reveal itself. Worse, as she stumbles over a log and knocks her head against a low branch, a delirious voice in her head tells her that she's been wandering these woods her entire life, searching for her lost husband.

"LAURA! TODD!" she yells, stumbling down an embankment and narrowly avoiding a tree trunk. "EDDIE!"

Voices join her own, rising like the forest itself—tree calling to tree, parent calling to child. They create a chorus of desperation; horrible, yes, but as long as they're calling to each other, they're still drawing breath. She can get to Eddie. She can fix this. She couldn't before, but this time she's ready for what lurks in the woods. She will not be thwarted by what the darkness hides.

Last time she wasn't ready. When she finally found her husband deep in the forest, all those years ago, she had barely made it out with her sanity, let alone her life. She wandered for what felt like hours, getting more desperate with each new shade of darkness leaking through the canopy.

She drifted, aimless, watching as twilight stained the sky with ink. She always thought these woods likely weren't that large. She'd never seen a map, but she got the impression that civilization crowded comfortably against the forest edges and that the woods were two, maybe three square miles.

But after walking for about an hour, the scale of the forest became harder and harder to quantify. No sounds beyond the natural noises of the coming night breached the forest walls: no cars, no people talking, no planes flying overhead. It was like she'd gone back in time, back before this land was conquered by modernity, back when the beasts held dominion over every inch of dirt. And as she considered her lonely predicament, something shifted.

She didn't hear it. It wasn't a sound. Sandy couldn't quite put a finger on what it was exactly. Maybe a sudden temperature drop, or a fluctuation in barometric pressure. Whatever the change, it made her come to an abrupt halt on the trail. She turned, curious, brow-furrowed, and peered deep into the thick underbrush. Night was fast approaching; leaving the trail was a good way to ensure she slept under a tree. But there was something there. A great susurration of the air. It rippled through the trees and burrowed deep into her skull, trying and failing to scratch a deep itch. It made her head feel fuzzy. Thoughts were caught in its strange netting before they could fully form. Without really recognizing what she was doing, Sandy stepped off the trail.

Now, there is no trail. There is no light. The only sounds are the crunching of branches beneath her feet, her own panicked breathing, and the occasional shout of one of her family. As she staggers through the forest, however, their voices dwindle around her, sinking into the folds of night, until the only sound is of her own frenzied progress. She stops moving and leans against a tree sticky with sap, breathing hard, one hand clutching at her chest. It's cold. Late autumn is beginning to crisp at the edges with frost; there's no way anyone could survive out here night after night in the frigid dark. Certainly not a baby.

The thought is horrible in its obvious simplicity. She staggers backward, falling hard against the trunk of a maple. How could she have been so stupid? Even if William hasn't already devoured Danny, how could she have thought an infant would survive for so long without proper care? The idea now feels like a foreign object in her skull, a sharp twig poking into her brain, just behind the eyes. Not her thought at all. She makes a gasping, maniacal sort of laugh. The night air eats it like a ripe peach. This is her fault. Now she has joined the ranks of the men in her life, failing them just as thoroughly as they failed her. Todd screams for Eddie from some part of the forest where there is still hope.

All those years ago, as she crashed through the underbrush toward the energy radiating deep in the trees, she had felt something like moral superiority. Here she was, going out into the forest to drag her husband back by the scruff of his neck—the only one in the family willing (or capable) of doing what needed to be done. But as she got deeper into the woods and the sky darkened by degrees, that delicious self-righteousness was replaced by mounting unease. Finding the trail again would be difficult, certainly, but that wasn't her main concern. Her main concern was a more fundamental flavor of 'Lost': the further she strayed from the trail, the more convinced she was of her literal displacement. The trees grew crooked and scabby, large areas of their trunks bare of bark, revealing dark, slimy wood beneath. The ground beneath her feet was too yielding, spongy almost, and she felt as if the earth released her every step only grudgingly and would perhaps change its mind on her next footfall. Meanwhile, the rippling sensation had grown almost to a point past bearing. It thrummed inside her like the heartbeat of a serpent, and with it came a deep, almost sexual ache. With each step, she felt certain the next would leave her a trembling ball on the forest floor.

And that's when she heard it: running water.

The snap of a twig. An intake of breath.

"Grandma?" Sandy peers through the fog of her memory and it dissipates in an instant. Eddie stands before her, dirty, scratched, and bruised. But alive. His face is pale—a tiny moon in the late night of her days.

Sobbing and shaking in equal measure, she lurches toward him and enfolds him in her arms. He is stiff and cold. Were it not for his breath against her cheek and the wild vibration of his heart, she might be holding a corpse.

"How . . . how . . . how . . . ?" Sandy moans between hiccupping breaths.

Eddie grips her, quivering.

"He dropped me," he croaks. "He moved his head like he heard something and- and- and- he just, he- he- he-"

Sandy hears the onset of hyperventilation and maybe even a panic attack in his voice and all at once she remembers who she is. She seizes him like a life preserver and hefts him with more strength than she should be capable of. The fog is gone. The panic is gone. Her family is lost in the woods. No one's going to get them back but her.

"Eddie, listen to me," she says. She holds him awkwardly, one arm under him like he's an overgrown toddler. His legs dangle at his sides, almost scraping against the forest floor. His head is buried in the crook of her neck, taking in ever shallower breath. She puts her free hand to the back of his head. "Nod if you're hearing me, Eddie." His tiny skull shifts in her palm. "I need you to be brave for me. Brave for your Grandma." She begins to walk without really knowing where she's going, pulled by something past reason. "I shouldn't ask it of you. You've been brave enough for ten lifetimes. This is my fault, Eddie. I was stupid to ask this of you, I'm sorry, I'm so sorry." His breathing has slowed. It's almost like they only have enough composure between them to accommodate one at a time, passing it back and forth as the moment demands. Sandy clears her throat and exhales a whistling breath. "Which way did he go?"

Eddie cocks a thumb over his shoulder—an oddly casual gesture—in the direction he came, the direction she's going. Sandy makes her way forward through the crackling leaves, her grandson held like a shield against the night.

When she had heard that sound all those years ago, she thought perhaps she had finally gone mad. Water does not simply appear. The earth does not block up and bleed like the skin of something mortal. Running water breaking new ground is a slow, methodical process, too diligent to be witnessed by the impatient eyes of humanity. She staggered through unfriendly branches and cloying, abandoned spiderwebs and scoffed at the impossibility. But there it was, gurgling through her ears.

She followed the sound blindly. There were only two things in this forest: she and her husband. It was a truth so fundamental; she did not question it. Anything she came across was inextricably linked to one of them, a part of them. And the water was not of her.

This logic wriggled like a maggot in her brain. Perhaps it was born of desperate anxiety and fear, but there was also the undeniable seed of truth in its belly. The truth being she had it exactly right: the forest was not of her, but it was of William. Or William was of it. So too the water, and the thick, sludgy night air. She had stumbled into a place outside the natural order, and she felt the queasy scrutiny of a virus under a microscope. Soon, antibodies would descend.

She almost stepped in it. Her foot hovered in the air over the glossy surface, and she only pulled it back when she caught the flash of her own eyes in what appeared to be shimmering earth. She stumbled a little as she stepped away from the bank.

The water was wide. A song from her childhood occurred to her—an insipid little melody that made her feel mocked and bullied. And it made the vision before her all the more horrible. She could see the other side of the bank, but just barely. A vast, lonely swath of air stretched out in all directions, bereft of trees. A constant, sibilant sigh whispered through the night. It was not the small stream that her daughter-in-law would see decades later, but a mighty river, flowing with the calm, certain determination of a thing that had lived longer than Sandy's species had stood upright. Things moved just beneath the water's surface. Long, patient shadows.

Sandy tore her eyes away. This. This was the water that William spoke of. And for the first time, she caught a glimpse of the path to his madness: the water was deep. There was much and more to be found below its surface. Perhaps the only thing that kept Sandy from kneeling and peering into the water until something rose to meet her was the knowledge of the price the water took. It was a black hole, gathering celestial bodies into its endless maw. She made a sharp right and followed the river's progress. She didn't have to go far.

Sandy crested a rise and stopped. Ahead: light. Pale blue. Like the coming dawn. She broke into a run.

The river curved sharply, vanishing behind the crowd of the forest. She slowed, the vibrations of the air almost lifting her off her feet with each pulse. She got lower—the act of something small attempting to get smaller in the presence of something too large. A long dormant instinct. She inched around the river's edge, her progress slowed by branches. The light grew and blossomed into the empty air.

Luckily for Sandy, her brain shielded her from fully remembering the next two minutes. In dreams she'll catch snatches of it, like a familiar song from a passing car. And for the rest of her life, certain small things will be enough to set her on edge: waterfalls, cephalopods, men moaning. She'll never quite understand why. Because when Sandy saw the water itself move above the shore, it took a part of her. When she saw her husband, hanging spread eagle in the air, naked and convulsing, the water holding him aloft, any lasting affection for him scurried away like frightened rats into a sewer. And when she saw the sky torn open to reveal a red, muscley morass dotted with scores of unblinking eyes, her hair went white at the temple. Every moment, she forgot what she was seeing, and unearthed the horror again. An endless loop of hideous discovery.

When she finally fell back through the bushes, she instantly forgot most of what she had seen. She ran anyway.

But now, Sandy can feel her brain preparing for the memory to return. She hitches Eddie against her shoulder, and he taps her back: *let me down.* She puts him back on his feet and cups his face. His eyes are shining, but they're clear. His breath is even.

"You're doing great," she says gruffly.

He shakes his head. "No, I'm not," he says. "Something's wrong with mom."

Sandy feels her skin break out into goosebumps. "What do you mean?" Her whisper is harsh and dusty.

Eddie hugs himself and looks around. The trees huddle close. She cannot tell if they're neighbors or strangers.

"I saw her after Grandpa dropped me," he whispers. His eyes have grown wide and unseeing. "She—she walked right past me. I yelled to her, but she—she didn't even look at me." Now his eyes dart up and meet Sandy's own. They are bright with wonder and terror. "She was following Grandpa."

A noise pierces the night, so unexpected that Sandy does not at first recognize it. But then her mother's organ stirs and Eddie sighs—the breath of found redemption. They take off after the sound of Danny's shrieking as it tears the night asunder.

V. THE PANTRY

TO FEED AND be full.

It is the simple, singular need of the creature crashing through the forest underbrush. A thread tugging at him, tangled in it as he stumbles and jerks deeper into the forest. The hunger. It is the one truth, and it guides him as arteries guide disease.

The brain of the creature that was once William is black and rotting. Maggots from another world wriggle through his gray matter, animating his limbs and feeding him words like a puppeteer from the shadows above a proscenium. He can feel each one as they probe his frayed nerve endings and eat the dead tissue that once held thought.

Food squirms in his grip. Food or Evan. The word—*Evan*—is not a name, as it once was. It is a designation; an office. The creature's previous Evan had been slurped back into that world of which the creature holds only dim, cloudy memories. He taught the Evan how to feed him, though he wanted to eat it very badly—that is, until the Evan curdled into a stinking, bony human. It was easier then.

Tall things scream. They stumble and stagger away from the creature, dropping to wooden knees, hollows turning to gaping, screaming mouths as they pass. All the poking, twisted arms shy away and even the ground tries to hide from him. There is a small bit of brain, untouched by the wriggling intruders, that is almost hurt by the forest's horror of him. He is not to be feared. He is the one being chased.

Chased. Yes. That's why he's running. Chased by the Evan's humans and the other one. The one that is short like food but would, the creature knows, taste like ashes. The creature's mind lingers, momentarily untethered from his propulsive hunger. She flashes in his mind like sunlight off glass and his squalling thoughts continue to drift toward her, fascinated by something in his fetid brain that is not about food. She had said something to him. It had glowed in the dark air and it was beautiful, soft, and familiar. The maggots shift. They swarm and feed on the vestigial tissue. No need for that. Sandy's face fades with each bite.

Soon, he will feed. Now that he has the Evan, he can eat the smallest—the grandson. The word has no meaning for the creature; it's just a sound, correct and intelligible as a scream. It will taste very good, even though it's gotten smaller and it stinks quite badly. It still moves when the creature touches it, but less with every year. Or second. He's forgotten how time moves—or if it stays still and he moves through it. Strictly speaking, he doesn't know time. His existence is a single white, hot ball of hunger—the universe the instant before the Big Bang.

The water showed him. The water showed him the hunger. A thick curtain was pulled around it; no one else was allowed to see. But the water had pulled it back to reveal the crackling, warm beauty that makes everything move. It showed him because he was special and he deserved to see. Even now, when the hunger is the only electricity able to contract his rotting muscles, he loves it. It swims sweet through his veins.

With each stuttering step, the creature forgets a little more about his pursuers until he is walking calmly and the Evan jerks ever frailer in his grip. Friendly, delicious dark enfolds him, guiding him back to the grandson.

"First, don't let them see," the creature croaks; the beginning of an old and deep-etched set of commandments. Like with most things, the meaning behind it is lost, only understood as the recipe for his meals. "Second, the smaller the better. They are weaker and they are juicier." Instantly, his mouth starts watering. A thin stream of drool oozes from his lips and plops onto the Evan. "Third, bring it to Dad as soon as you have it. Do not hide, or delay. If they chase you, Daddy will hide you better."

The forest is no longer hiding. It welcomes him with oozing arms. Any lingering concern about his safety fizzles like matches in water. Home. The Sleeping Place. *Pantry.* That last word dangles like a hook before his eyes, the way all words do that once held a specific connotation for the creature. The memory of its association is long gone. The part of his brain that held the memory—Sandy, Todd, and Evan giggling in the pantry after a sack of flour had burst, showering William in powdery white—was eaten in the early days of his devouring. But the word *pantry* . . . it still carries with it the sheen of affection, though the creature doesn't know that's what it is. He is merely drawn to the word, and is vaguely aware of its association to food.

There is one tree that the creature returns to again and again. It sits at the heart of the forest, an enormous Lord of peeling black bark and dripping blood. It is a beacon of sorts. It emits a tantalizing scent that works its way into the brains of everything it can reach, and pulls each one to its base. Even the other trees around it bow in its direction—subjects before their liege. The reasons for its beckoning belong only to the Lord. For most creatures caught in its snare merely stop before it, stare for a time, and wander off to see to their own strange business.

The creature once known as William doesn't know any of this. In the Pantry, he is never required to consider the "why" of anything, but merely follows the voice of each thing that beckons, and so returns to the Black Lord time and time again.

Oh.

But there is another voice. The oldest voice he knows; his dearest and only friend. With only the dimmest awareness, he drops his arms and the Evan falls to the ground with a weak cry.

The water. It's been so very long—hours, at least years. And it's calling to him. He follows the roaring from somewhere further out among the forest.

Tall things bend away from him; not in fear, but in deference, their black, wasted bodies parting to guide him to the water's edge. The sky above leaks shadow. The ground beneath him shudders and sighs at his touch. There is someone walking beside him.

The creature turns his head, momentarily startled out of his fixation. The word *daughter* drifts through his squirming mind, but that's not correct. It's a human, he knows one when he sees it. In an indistinct way, he even knows that he used to be one, though it's the same way humans know that they were babies: I was something before; it must have been this.

The human turns her head to look at him and he immediately recognizes fear in her features. But he sees something else, too. That familiar ebb and flow behind her irises. The water. The water has her.

With this understanding, a righteous and beautiful jealousy erupts through him—beautiful because it is so foreign to his mind—and he lunges for her, meaning to bite. His teeth feel too big in his mouth, like they're swollen from disuse. The water is for him, only him. It *belongs* to him. Or he belongs to the water. Either way, she intrudes.

His jaw snaps inches from her ear as she staggers away from him. A black trunk catches her, throws her roughly back into the path of divining. She makes a sound, a low *huhn!* and breaks into a shambling run. The creature's shriveled heart lurches. He bows his head, preparing to charge. She will not reach the water first. But he can smell it now, it's very close. The sound of it fills the forest. Ahead, he catches a glint of pale moonlight leaping from the surface. It has begun to rain. Hot, stinging droplets on his exposed skin. The creature lunges.

She crumples beneath his weight. Something snaps and it sends a luscious shock through his middle as they crash into thick, cloying mud. He grunts against her neck. The breath is forced from her body. For a few heartbeats, they grapple together on the ground in the quickly sludging soil. He feels his nails catching wet flesh, but they only graze atop the surface. Her legs are thrust against his chest, keeping him from fully claiming her. He swats them away, and he falls upon her.

A cracking sound fills his head and he falls to his side. The world swirls, then crashes into focus. With it comes the pain, and the creature makes a sound somewhere between a moan and a scream. He hits the ground as a rock lands in the mud an inch from his face.

The human is crawling away. Away toward the water. Through the thick veil of pain and the hissing deluge, he can see it, beckoning. He manages to get to his knees, then his feet. He sways and the world sways with him. The moon fills its own corner of the sky and grins with chalky teeth upon the screaming black river below. Long, bristly shadows break the surface and leer upon the human as she crawls ever closer.

The creature takes a hesitant step, then another. She's reaching for something. A shock shudders through him. The curtain is about to be pulled.

All at once, he's charging her. The water glows, and he can see her face. She's gotten to her knees, one arm stretched over the water's edge. The curtain twitches.

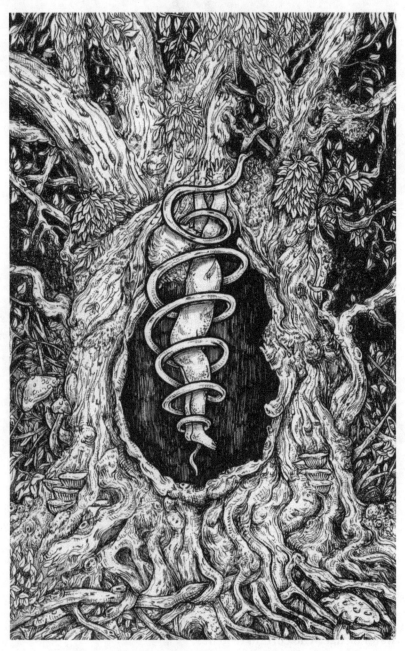

In the perfect dark of the tree hollow

VI. THE BLACK LORD

THE FABRIC BETWEEN worlds strains and snaps.

Todd is the first pursuer to breach it, tearing pell-mell after his father and son through the forest that bleeds seamlessly from one world to another. When he slips through this barrier, he doesn't notice, except for a passing recognition that the temperature has dropped considerably. He doesn't slow.

Next comes Laura, a bundle of crackling panic, tearing blindly through the underbrush, passing through the chasm in space-time with a single pulsing thought: "*Not again, not again, not again.*"

Last is Sandy. She too feels it when she enters this new plane, but she doesn't register that this is what transpires. Only the flood of memories marks her passage, her sense memory triggered like a deer at the sound of a gunshot.

Of the humans that pass into this unfamiliar world, Eddie is the only one who sees; the only one who understands. As his grandfather bears him into darkness, Eddie's eyes tilt upward toward the night sky, seeking help from a God that he suddenly understands—in some deep, unspoken part of himself—does not exist. When they break through the barrier never meant to be broken, the sky shifts. The uniform familiar black ripples, as if it's not the sky at all, but the surface of some vast, alien ocean. Stars shudder, flicker, go out. The heavens convulse, undulating and spiraling, black in some places, a deep violent purple in others. Splashes of color that Eddie can't name mix and swirl around celestial bodies that could be stars, but seem too close; he can see their fire. His grandfather slows to a jog, then a trot, and his muscles relax. His grip loosens. And Eddie knows he's farther from home than he's ever been, or ever will be.

Deep at the center of the dark wood, the branches of the Black

Lord twitch, as if in a breeze. It feels in the way all ancient things feel: a shift in the sameness of its surroundings, a recognition of alteration. New energy. The Lord calls to this new energy, and feels resistance from within and without. There is a struggle in its kingdom and it has everything to do with the dying creature buried in the hollow of its trunk. A root emerges from the soil, probing in the darkness toward the bundle of warmth. It hesitates. Perhaps it beholds the child, wrapped in a filthy blanket, far smaller than it should be, and perhaps it feels pity, or sorrow. Whatever the reason for its lingering, it doesn't last. The root pulls back, and lashes the child's face, whip-like, leaving a pink welt across Danny's cheek. He inhales sharply, and a moment later he's squalling harder than he has since his birth. The root retreats back into the fetid soil, sated.

Danny's wailing cuts through the silence like a blade through flesh. Deeper in the forest, Sandy and Eddie hear his cries and set out with new purpose. They don't know it yet, but they are not the only ones who hear. The trees hide things that scrabble and lurk, peering from shadows, assessing, listening. What they hear could be a threat, it could be a meal.

Eddie leads his grandmother, lured by his brother's squalling, but also by the inexorable pull of the Black Lord exerting its pressure, tugging invisible strings. Eddie senses this power at work, chooses not to articulate it.

His grandmother feels it as well, but a shift has occurred sometime between when they first heard Danny's crying and now: she's no longer in charge. This is Eddie's task; it's now her job to see that he succeeds. With this understanding comes a wave of relief, followed closely by guilt over her relief. She is the adult, after all, and so much has been put on this child already. She should be ceding no control, shouldn't be looking to him for guidance. But as she watches Eddie, striding with haste and purpose through the clinging branches and cloying soil, she can't bring herself to deny this simple, self-evident fact. Eddie needs to save Danny. She can only help, whatever that might mean.

For his part, Eddie is barely aware of anything except his brother's continued crying and the strange tugging sensation behind his ribcage. Grandma is close behind him and he can feel her scanning their surroundings, checking shadows. Danny pauses in his wailing, and the night lapses into silence. Another cry breaks it, but this one stops Eddie in his tracks and Sandy almost crashes into him.

"What is it?" she asks, eyes straining through the darkness ahead of them. Eddie's breathing has become shallow and raspy, an old man's wheeze. She grips his shoulder.

"That's not Danny," Eddie whispers. "Listen."

Sure enough, the cry comes again, and Sandy is overcome with a kind of auditory vertigo as Danny's weeping is overlaid with another, nearly identical wail; a mocking, almost gleeful imitation, stuttering near the end into what sounds like cackling.

"Oh, Jesus," says Sandy, grip tightening on Eddie's shoulder.

"Something's copying him," Eddie says, and resumes walking, as if this is not something that should make him turn and run until he's safely under the covers back at his house.

Sandy feels a horrible chill pass through her as she stumbles forward, following her grandson's lead.

✳ ✳ ✳

In another part of the forest, Todd has slowed to a shambling jog, out of breath, nearly delirious with fatigue and fear. He has to stop, there's no way around it. Running blindly through the woods isn't going to get Eddie or Danny back. He lost track of his father's movements a long time ago, has continued running because of inertia alone. He slows, trips over a jutting root, and leans against a tree for support.

Immediately, he yanks his hand away with a hiss of disgust. The tree's bark is slick and slimy with a strange viscous substance. He holds his palm close to his face, trying to see better by the meager moonlight. It shimmers, smells like blood. It's starting to burn.

Todd whimpers and wipes his palm hastily on his pant leg. For the first time, he takes in his surroundings. The trees bend at odd, seemingly impossible angles. The soil beneath his feet is soft, almost buoyant. When he looks up at the swirling night sky, stars burning in and out of existence, he finally understands.

He tries calling for Eddie, for Laura, for his mother. But his lungs won't let him pull in enough air, and so his screams come out as croaks. All around him, trees bend close, branches clattering, though there's no wind that he can feel. Maybe the trees here aren't trees at all. They seem sentient, mobile things that could uproot and descend upon him at any moment. He rummages in his pocket, searching for the gun, and freezes. It's gone. Lost sometime during the sanity-crushing chase. The last hope, swallowed by the forest.

Todd puts his head in his hands and drops to his knees. The soil pulls greedily at his legs, cold and damp. *An early grave,* he thinks, and that's about what he deserves. His failure is insurmountable. It's the massive wall that surrounds him on all sides; unscalable, his eventual tomb. His most fundamental trait as a father, as a husband, as a son, as a brother.

But there is a small grace: there's nothing left to ruin. He can be done now, if he wants to be. Do no more damage, suffer no more sorrow. He lets gravity do its work and he falls forward, plunging into the dirt, and now he's almost completely submerged. Almost completely buried. The soil smells like an open wound.

Here Todd lies, for a time. How long is hard to say. Time moves sluggishly in this world, lingering when it should fly. But over the course of minutes, maybe hours, he becomes aware of something besides his slowly sinking body and the smell of death. A pale blue light, leaking through the dirt and through the gaps between his fingers. Todd opens his eyes.

Sitting up is a nearly herculean effort. Todd had been completely swallowed by the stinking earth, and getting to his knees turns out to be an almost failing struggle. But this, at least, Todd succeeds at. The weight of the soil sloughs off him in cascades as he tries to stand, staggers, and rights himself. Yes, there is a light. Somewhere deep among the forest, making the tree's silhouettes look like a long, crooked fence. It's not daylight. It's something else.

All at once, Todd is running again, his failure forgotten. The light grows.

✷✷✷

Somewhere outside the light's influence, the Black Lord bends over the creatures as they enter the clearing at its roots. Eddie and Sandy slow, caught somewhere between awe and terror.

"That," Sandy says, neck craning, "is a big tree."

"Is it?" Eddie asks. "A tree, I mean."

Sandy doesn't answer. She thinks probably not, but she's not fully prepared for the ramifications of that. The squalling takes up again. It's coming from the base of the tree, echoing as if Danny is deep in a cavern. Eddie spares the looming branches one last glance. He's pretty sure they're moving up there, black against black. But Eddie doesn't sense danger in this. The feeling he has reminds him of a zoo, only not from the perspective he's used to.

"Let's go," Grandma says, right at his ear. "I want to get your parents and leave." Eddie moves forward without another word.

As they approach, they make out an enormous dark shape at the tree's base. A hollow, almost ten feet tall, like a cave opening. Even in the weak moonlight, Eddie can see that the soil around it is padded down, hardened by the frequent movement of feet. He breaks into a run.

A cry comes from somewhere to his left, now only passingly similar to his brother's. Eddie freezes. Behind him, Sandy stops too, once again gripping his shoulder. Eddie peers into the shadows, eyes tuned to movement. There's a shift behind the dense tree line. Darkness peeling away from darkness.

When Sandy was a girl, she spent a summer with her parents in India. She doesn't remember much about it beyond the heat and the smell of spices. Brilliant colors on both the people and the flora. The single, specific memory she holds is of standing on the veranda of their hotel room, watching a mongoose and a cobra grapple in the grass below her. Before she understood that they were fighting, Sandy had been convinced the two creatures were playing. The snake had been wound around the mongoose as it jumped back and forth, like it was dancing. It had been strange, mesmerizing. Oddly graceful. And then the mongoose had gotten the snake's throat between its teeth, and the moment became hideous. This is what comes to Sandy now. First a mongoose, then a cobra, then that moment before first blood. The frenzied dance emerging into the clearing beneath the gargantuan not-a-tree.

The thing opens its mouth—Eddie sees with a thrill of revulsion that it has the face of a man—and lets forth another squall, prickly around the edges, like it's choking on the sound. Then it collapses into cackling, writhing forward toward the hollow.

"No," Eddie tries to say, but the sight has knocked the wind out of him.

The creature lurches, and Sandy sees the white flicker of teeth. It squirms, its many feet scrabbling through the dirt, bee-lining toward the hollow.

Sandy takes a step, then another, a half-concocted plan to charge the beast held in her mind. But then Eddie grabs her wrist, and she turns to him. He points up. She blinks, then turns just in time to see a branch, easily four feet across, sweep down from the sky in a neat arc, connecting with the creature feet away from the hollow. There's a wet crunching, and a yelp that sounds alarmingly like a kicked dog, and the creature is sailing through the air, high enough to clip the treetops. A moment later, the sound of snapping branches and a very definitive thud.

A few heartbeats pass, Sandy and Eddie both locked in a sort of incredulous amazement. The Black Lord's branch arcs back the way it came, all ease and grace, and returns to its stationary position. There's a sensation of anticipation, of waiting for something to happen, and Sandy realizes the feeling comes not from them, but from the tree itself. She gently pushes Eddie forward.

"It's safe," she whispers, though she hadn't known she was going to say this until the words left her lips. But as soon they do, she knows she's right.

The hollow seems to grow as they approach. Danny has stopped crying, but Eddie can make out his soft whimpering breath. *He's cried himself out*, Eddie thinks. It's not the first time he's had this thought. In the early days of Danny's life, his brother had cried and cried and cried. Hours after Eddie's mom and dad had brought him home, he had finally stopped crying and this is what his dad had said: *He's cried himself out*. His dad's words echoed in Eddie's head every time his family got that brief reprieve. And in those early days, every time he stopped crying, Eddie had tiptoed into Danny's nursery, intent on making sure he was okay. And every time, he was. Sleeping an untroubled sleep. Perfect, unharmed.

Eddie can stand it no longer. He starts running again. Sandy, startled, doesn't have the chance to stop him, and so takes off after him. The smell inside the tree is rich and blessedly familiar. The smell of a forest; wood and soil.

"Danny?" Eddie calls, and drops to his hands and knees,

terrified of stepping on his brother. His voice echoes strangely around him. "Danny, where are you?" There's a sound, a weak coo from somewhere to Eddie's left. Eddie cries out and paws his way through the dirt, calling Danny's name as he goes.

And then his hand finds fabric, filthy and bedraggled. Eddie gasps, and feels a sob swelling inside him. He moves his hands gently forward, pulling lightly at the blanket he remembers from Danny's crib. He remembers the feel, dirty and torn as it is. Zoo animals, smiling from the safety of cages. He scoops his hands under Danny's emaciated but breathing body and lifts the little swaddle of fading heat to his chest.

There he is. Somehow, in the perfect dark of the tree hollow, Eddie can see him. Blue eyes peering out of a thin, dirt-streaked face. Danny's tiny hand lifts and touches his brother's cheek.

Now, Eddie does cry. Deep, wailing sobs that reverberate through the hollow. He holds Danny tight, putting his face to his brother's. Danny doesn't seem to mind, and coos again. Eddie becomes aware of his grandma kneeling down behind them, embracing them both, crying along with him. The three of them cry and breathe, then quiet. There is a fullness here, a sense of completion. Eddie breathes in the smell of his brother's scalp. Even through the dirt, the smell is familiar. The smell of sunshine, of newness.

And then, abruptly, Eddie and Sandy are on their feet and running out of the hollow back into the forest, the Black Lord observing them as they run.

A maelstrom is brewing. They all feel it, coagulating above them, slow but inevitable. A poison electricity in the air. Sandy glances above as they run. The sky has turned a bruised purple, swollen with angry-looking clouds. A drop of rain hits her forehead, making her skin tingle, like the spot it hit has suddenly fallen asleep. She wipes the drop away and sees that it's not rain at all, but a dark, thick substance, slightly musty smelling. Moments later, all three of them are drenched in the stuff, the smell of a closed-off basement thick in their nostrils. Danny whimpers and Eddie pulls him tighter.

Sandy is the first to see it. The pale blue light. Her memory groans beneath the weight of its illumination.

"Eddie, Eddie, wait, slow down," she says, and Eddie comes to a reluctant halt. She points ahead of them. "Do you see it?" He follows the line of her finger.

"The light?" he asks.

"Yes, the light." A pause.

"I see it," he says, clearly anxious to keep moving.

But Sandy is rooted to the spot. A sense of intense deja vu has overtaken her. Or perhaps it's a premonition. Whichever it is, she knows that that way lies peril, likely sorrow. Her fear grips her anew and she takes an involuntary step back, her subconscious balking at unearthing the horrible thing it's hidden.

A small hand slips into hers. She tears her eyes from the light to see Eddie, but not the child she's gotten to know so much better in these last couple days. No, it's the Eddie she knows she'll never see, the man who he'll become long after she's dead. World-weary, badgered by children of his own maybe. But determined. Unwavering. And Sandy has the sudden realization that she was wrong. Todd didn't fail her. Not by a long shot.

"Mom and dad," Eddie says, and that's all she needs. They set off again, but slower now, deferential to what waits for them.

✳✳✳

Less than a hundred yards away, Laura stands, staring at the soft blue light. It looks like daylight. It looks like home. There's something she's supposed to be doing, she knows that. She can even catch hold of the edges of the panic she knows she's supposed to feel. But all clear thought, all sense of purpose . . . it's drifted away into the night. The only really important thing is that beautiful, blue gleam. Without telling her legs to move, she's walking toward it.

Laura Sutner, trapped in the back of her own mind, is screaming. Perfect understanding at what awaits her sits like a hot, polished gem in her skull. But it's locked behind a door, down a deserted hall in the back room of her mind. And all she can hear, all that she's permitted to hear, is the soft, soothing voice of the water.

She stumbles onto a trail. No, not really a trail. There are no trails in this place. The trees have parted like Moses' Red Sea, and of course there's no way to go but toward the light. There's such wonder waiting for her that way. Rain pelts her, making her skin tingle pleasantly. And over the soft pitter-patter, she can hear the gentle roar of the water. A smile creases her cheeks. It's going to be better soon.

She doesn't realize there's someone beside her until teeth clamp shut so close to her face that she can smell her father-in-law's stinking breath.

***

Todd watches this and the following struggle as if he's in a dream, standing stupidly just outside the path of divining. When his father tries to take a bite out of Laura, he takes a step forward, but it's like trying to walk into a wall of speakers blasting heavy metal. He stumbles backward, crying out in frustration. It's lost in the roar of the storm. All he can do is walk just outside of the path of the parted trees, watching his wife and father's progress, panic rising in his gullet like vomit.

It can't happen. He can't let it happen. He won't let his father take anyone else from his family. He takes another step and nearly loses his balance. He pitches forward and sees his own blue eyes reflected in the water. At the last moment, he catches a branch—or does it catch him?—and he pulls himself back to the bank.

The water. Ahead of him, as far as he can see in every direction, flowing, angry rapids. How had he not heard it until now; that furious roaring, drinking the rain like a monstrous beast dying of thirst? It should be impossible. The water is moving too fast to show him his reflection. But there it is. Gazing back at him from the black. Below his doppelganger, massive shadows churn. With an intense effort, he drags his gaze away.

Over the water at the end of the path of divining, a floating liquid shadow. Todd stares for a few heartbeats, his mind unable to lock onto any discreet edges, any true sense of form. All he knows is that it's not looking at him. Its attention is on the person kneeling at the water's edge. It's Laura, reaching toward the black.

***

It should be understood: the universe is mostly chaos. Forces working in tandem and in conflict, coalescing and clashing at random into outcomes unforeseen and unplanned. Every human can sense it on some level; many try to deny it, but the universe doesn't take any notice. Things happen, or they don't, and every event transpires without scheme.

The same cannot be said of the universe of the water, of the Black Lord, of the poison rain, and the greedy soil. Here, forces move in perfect conjunction. Every tree that grows, every corpse that rots, it's all to a singular purpose. Since the moment Eddie was first borne through the breach between worlds, machinery has been in motion. Without knowing it, each of the creatures who entered this world have been working together, working toward something. To this moment of confluence.

The threads of their actions twist like rope, and the Black Lord, the tree-that-is-not-a-tree, sees it all with perfect, delicious clarity. Its roots go deep in this world, and it feels every movement, every ripple of air, every anxious thought and understands what each one means, how it will guide another. It pulls on these threads, ties them, clips them at their root. To what end is unclear. Its purpose is beyond knowing, like trying to understand the mind of a planet. The best a human mind might be able to grasp is a kind of knowing hunger. Hunger and a sense of balance: one for one, the beast is fed.

And so, the Lord ties the threads together and waits.

✳✳✳

Eddie, Danny, and Sandy force their way onto the path of divining, witnesses to what is about to transpire. Laura reaches for the flapping fabric, inches from understanding. The creature charges her, its jealousy licking its insides like fire.

And Todd. His path opens before him like a flower opening to sun, and Todd is filled not with fear, or trepidation, or uncertainty. No, he feels only two things as he forces his way onto the path: the first is gratitude, a warm welcoming wave of it. He's been given the chance to fix it after all. The second, and the more powerful of the two, is love.

This is how Todd is able to smile as he shatters the water's repellent barrier and breaks into a sprint. Love for his family, and an understanding that he has, at long last, succeeded.

His body connects with the creature's, and from a distance, it could be an embrace: the ecstatic son greeting his long-lost father. But a moment later, gravity breaks the illusion. The creature makes a sound, inquisitive, as if it's spotted something strange on the horizon, and then they're tumbling backward, feet slipping at the water's edge.

There's a moment when Todd is suspended over the water. His eyes meet Laura's, her hypnosis broken, and she sees him fully. The water's grip on her has shattered, and for a few lovely moments, it's replaced with her husband's face.

Something passes between them. Laura will never be able to articulate it to herself, but for the rest of her life, she'll see his crooked, almost rueful smile; his eyes, brilliant shining blue. The face that communicates all that needs to be said the instant before it breaks the water's surface and vanishes beneath the waves.

✳✳✳

How they made it home, they would have all been hard pressed to answer, though Eddie has a sneaking suspicion it had to do with the tree, the one he's begun to think of as the Black Lord. He has a feeling as he and Sandy walk to Laura—still staring at the place Todd vanished, now nothing more than dark soil—like there's someone out there among the trees, watching them, keeping tabs. It's not a malevolent feeling. More akin to being subtly followed by a store clerk minutes before closing: *Time to go, please.*

In the moments after Todd and the creature broke through the water, there had been a sense of suspension. Sandy had pictured a key in a lock, turned all the way, the door about to be pushed open. And then the water was gone. She had sensed something pulse through the air as it vanished, hot and fetid, and she knew it instinctively for anger. A force had been thwarted here, though its direction is hard to pinpoint. This is, after all, not her world, and she reminds herself that none of this is familiar, that the trees are not trees, the rain is not rain, and the water is not water.

Laura, for her part, is still not fully awake. Passing from the long dream of the water to the brief flash of Todd's face had been like a sharp slap in the middle of a nightmare. She feels light-headed, strangely empty. There was something inside her that isn't there anymore, and though she's glad to be rid of it, there is a part of her that aches for it, for the sense of fullness. It reminds her how she felt after she had her children. A single tear rolls down her cheek as Sandy, Eddie and Danny walk up behind her. They linger there together, for a minute, an hour, or a day, until Laura gets to her feet, and they turn away from the spot Todd vanished.

When they see the light, no one says a thing. It's not the pale blue light of the water. They all know it for what it is: the soft, golden glow of morning. Through the trees, the breach becomes clear. A tear in the fabric of darkness, leaking light, trees bending to clear a path.

Danny emerges from his filthy blanket and blinks against the new light. He coos; a question, searching for a memory. Tiny fingers appear from beneath the rotted cloth, reaching toward the promise of warmth. His hand is the first thing the sunlight touches.

BONUS MATERIAL

Enjoy this additional short story from Colin Hinckley.

A MOUTH FILLED WITH
THE TEETH OF TREES

OLIVE DIDN'T SAY much as we left. The city receded in our rearview, a black and gray stain on the blue sky, and vanished from our lives without remark. She didn't say anything as we passed through the suburbs, said nothing of the monolithic drowsy calm, said nothing of how it reminded her of home. When we passed through a blurred cluster of anonymous small towns, "famous" for their doll museum or local nineteenth-century author's house, she dozed and I listened to public radio at the lowest volume, an anxious dread coiling and uncoiling in my chest. The countryside passed in a haze of early autumn color and the smell of that natural decay eased me somewhat, but I could never really get out from under it.

The dread, I mean. It made me feel guilty, too, in a roundabout sort of way. Clearly, Olive was in some kind of shell shock, in the throes of something a lot worse than my second-hand dread; I should be focused on her, not the sublime terror that her family's death had triggered in me.

Trees began to crowd right up to the edge of the road. Turns became sharper and pavement became patchier. I told myself (and not for the first time) that we had lucked out here. That fortune had given the two of us an escape hatch. A house, surprisingly cheap, half the rent of our apartment in New York, nestled away in the Vermont countryside. We weren't going to do much better than that.

Staying in the city had become unsustainable for many reasons, but the most pressing to my mind was the immediacy of what had happened, how *close* we were to it. It was like driving away from a blast zone, desperately trying to escape the shockwave. We had watched it happen from our fire escape. The moments immediately after, at least. The whole neighborhood had. I couldn't imagine waking up every day to that memory. So close. To have it leer at us from the street.

I turned the radio off, trying not to think about it too closely, trying not to think about how strange the fire had looked in the middle of the road or how the sound of rending metal seemed to hang in the air, as if it were a distortion in the ether not easily smoothed away. Olive shifted in her seat, sighed, and came lurching out of sleep, a whimper at the back of her throat. I reached out instinctively to touch her shoulder and she shied away. I pulled back, embarrassed and concerned, and looked at her sidelong.

"Okay?" I asked.

She nodded, then rolled down the window, poked her head out, and inhaled deeply. The wind whipped at her sweater, the same one she'd been wearing for a week or so—brown, too big for her; her father's sweater.

"Smells fresher here," she said as she sat back down.

"Yeah," I said, happy to talk, happy to hear her voice. "It's all the evergreens."

"There's so many," she said, swiveling her head to look out her window, the windshield, the rearview. "I've never seen this many trees all at once."

"Welcome to Tree Town," I said dryly, trying for a little humor.

She smiled vaguely and we lapsed back into silence.

The road twisted ahead of us and presently gave way to dirt. Other cars on the road were infrequent but every driver, without fail, raised a hand in greeting as we passed, as if they already knew us, had already accepted our presence as neighbors.

"I keep seeing the same tree," Olive said.

"Yeah, I think a lot of these forests only have three or four varieties."

"That's not what I meant."

I cocked my head at her, confused, but she was staring out the window.

"There it is again," she said, pointing. I craned my neck to see, but it was all just a blur of browns and reds and greens.

"A new friend, maybe," I said after a while. No smile for that one.

***

There was a storm our first night. The wind was unlike anything I'd heard in the city; a low, throbbing wail that waxed and waned but never fully abated. Rain fell for a time, stopped, then turned to hail before being swept back into the sky. At nightfall, Olive locked herself in our bedroom. When I knocked, she insisted she was okay, just tired, and wanted to take a nap. But I could hear her crying from the first floor, even over the sound of the wind.

Boxes lay stacked in haphazard piles; furniture was shoved into random corners; it looked like our old life had been regurgitated into this strange house from the gullet of some giant monster. I pictured Manhattan, enormous legs sprouting from Wall Street, from East Harlem and Riverside Park, staggering two hundred miles north to belch our tiny, broken family into this dusty, neglected corner of the world. The image made me feel uneasy. Lonely, too, though I couldn't say why.

I wandered around the house, listening to the wind and Olive as they mourned. I turned on all the lights I could, even the sickly pale overhead in the kitchen that made the room look like a rendering plant. The house was dirty. The landlord hadn't bothered to do a proper cleaning before we arrived. We had never even met the guy, didn't know anything about him beyond his name and that he owned the place. It had given me a queer sense of unreality as we approached the house, took the keys out of the mailbox, let ourselves in.

After the accident, there had been weeks of intense focus on both of us. Everyone in our lives seemed to be peeking around corners, climbing through our windows to say how sorry they were, offering help and solace, then drifting away to be replaced with another concerned aunt or friend or co-worker. But now . . . we had been allowed to shift our entire lives without so much as a handshake. I think it was better for Olive. She had begun to talk—at least to me—once the hubbub of collective mourning had dissipated. But it left me feeling exposed. I didn't have the slightest idea how to keep her head above water.

On the staircase: a window. It looked out onto our small backyard and, further on, the forest. In daylight, I was sure it would be a pleasant view. But the storm made the forest look like a crowd of impatient giants jostling each other to get a better look at us. The wind dragged its fingers through branches, tossed leaves in great, billowing bundles, and made the canopy lurch and clatter against a sky filled with the smoke of storm clouds. The effect was unpleasant, otherworldly. There was no light except for the weak bulb over the back door; shadows darted through the pallid glow, giving the forest brief faces. Proximity to nature had always unnerved me. I preferred the recognizable order of humanity—cities, highways, department stores. Those I understood completely. I didn't understand the forest, didn't understand the weather that seemed to creep indoors, or the deceptive silence of the night between gales of wind. It felt alive in a way I wasn't ready for.

Something else, too. Something about the way the forest shifted that drew my eye off to the left. The way the shadows of trunks moved, the way they didn't. I squinted and leaned closer to the window. Among the swaying silhouettes of the trees, one stood unmoved by the tempest. The effect was almost kaleidoscopic. For a few heartbeats, I was gripped by the overwhelming sensation of falling down a pit, hurtling towards that unnatural, unmoving nexus; swallowed by a mouth filled with the teeth of trees.

I staggered backward and nearly slipped on the stairs. Above me, the bed groaned in its frame. I heard the boards creak beneath Olive's weight as she walked to the door and opened it. She stepped into the smudgy half-light and blinked down at me from the doorway. Her eyes were red and she appeared shriveled; she had a wrung-out quality to her.

"What are you doing?" she asked.

I looked out the window and pointed. "There was, uh . . . " But the forest had returned to its familiar, natural motion: parallel swaying shadows. " . . . a tree," I finished, feeling a bit stupid.

Olive gazed at me for a few seconds, then sighed.

"Yeah," was all she said, then walked down the hall and closed the bathroom door behind her.

✳✳✳

That night, I had a dream.

I was lost in the forest, and another storm was bearing down upon me. I could hear Olive singing somewhere in the foliage. I could see flashes of her white nightgown, but every time I ran toward her, she vanished between the trunks of the trees. Her song trailed behind her like a scent of perfume, mysterious and alluring, an alien melody. After searching for what felt like hours, I finally found her in an open field. Her arms were spread and she was gazing at the sky. As I watched, she slowly rose from the ground, the storm inviting her ever higher, until she vanished from my sight.

✳✳✳

What do you say to someone whose reality is shattered?

What even *is* reality for someone who went through what Olive went through? I couldn't help but feel like I was little more than a mirage to her; another specter conjured up by the liminal dream space she had stumbled into, caught somewhere between the mundane and the hellacious. It was surreal. The way she looked at me—sometimes like I was a mildly interesting movie, sometimes like I was a stranger who had wandered too close—was unsettling. I tried to remind myself that it wasn't about me, that I was a supporting actor in this particular episode. But, to my great shame, I found myself feeling dejected and put out by the unrelenting stupor of Olive's new existence. It was callous, and I knew it was callous, so I tried to keep it to myself. But after two weeks with barely more than ten words spoken between us, I let the frustration get the better of me.

"Are you going to do anything today besides lie in bed?" I asked. I was standing in the doorway, seized by a fierce sense of self-righteousness that had begun to seep away before the question was even out of my mouth.

Olive lifted her head and blinked at me in dull surprise. "Did you want to do something?" she asked. Sunlight was slicing through a gap in the curtains, cutting a line across her face; a scar made of light. I slumped in the doorway, deflated.

"No, I'm sorry," I said and walked to the bed. I sat, making the frame squeak. She watched me from her spot on the pillow, but I didn't see much behind her eyes. She was elsewhere. "I'm worried about you, Tini," I said, calling her by the pet name I hadn't used since before the accident. The provenance of that particular name was simple, but silly: olives go in martinis, thus Tini. In the old days, it would have produced a sardonic smile and maybe a playful punch on the arm. Now, she showed no sign that she had heard me.

"I think the woods are haunted," she said vaguely. Like she was saying she thought the roof might be leaking. The hair on the back of my neck prickled, but I shook the feeling away, annoyed with myself.

"That so?" I asked, careful not to let my incredulity show. I read somewhere that you shouldn't disagree with people who are grieving. That it just makes things worse. I might be thinking of dementia, though.

Olive nodded.

"Yeah," she said, though she didn't seem at all frightened by the prospect.

Outside, I heard the fluttering of birds, perhaps a flock of crows startled into flight. Of course, given the topic of conversation, I was tempted to ask myself a question: *startled by what?*

I waited for her to elaborate, but she just stared through the gap in the curtain, like she could see something through it other than the sun, already sinking low behind the treetops.

"Did . . . why do you think that?" I asked.

Her eyes flitted over to me with an expression that said *C'mon. You know.* But I didn't, so I just smiled.

"What's for dinner?" she asked. Again, I had to push down a surge of frustration. Was that all I was now? Chef and caretaker? The guardian of the bereaved? I quelled the voices, once more disgusted with myself.

"Anything you like," I said, intent on correcting my own internal petulance. She looked at me again, but this time I caught something strange in her glance. Disappointment? Disdain? Then, she rolled away, her back towards me.

"Not hungry," she mumbled, and said no more.

I sat there for a time, staring at her back, watching it rise and fall. The rhythm of her breath eventually became such that I knew she was sleeping, and I sighed. I looked toward the gap in the window, now a shimmering golden wire. The light made my eyes ache, but pleasantly so. When I closed them, the warmth of the setting sun felt like a physical presence in the room. Just another concerned friend, lingering for fear of catastrophe. The light went out. I opened my eyes, startled, as the room transitioned from gloom back to amber.

I stared at the gap, willing it to stay lit, to continue offering its fading glow. When all light had gone, I went downstairs to make dinner.

✳✳✳

Sleep had become scarce. During the night, at least. Olive would often sleep for large swaths of the day, then wander the house at night, leaving me uncomfortably conscious for long stretches of time. At night, when Olive was absent and sleep was elusive, I found that my grip on reality grew tenuous. It was difficult not to dwell on what Olive had said, about what I had seen in the stairwell window. Things easy to dismiss during the day became more credible at night. Shadows were deeper after dark, sounds were amplified. And though we were on the second floor, a strange certainty periodically gripped me: despite its obvious impossibility, I could often swear I saw someone walking past our bedroom window.

It was worse when a storm was passing through, which was often. I had never lived in the countryside; I had no idea how usual or unusual this was. But there seemed to be a storm every third or fourth night, like it was all the same storm, dropping into the valley before climbing back up the hillside to drench us before we'd even fully dried from its last visitation.

The growling thunder made me anxious. It was too easy to imagine some lumbering beast stalking us, the periodic snapping of branches marking its passage through the forest. I sat up. Olive was somewhere in the house, though if she was moving, I couldn't track her progress. The wind was too loud. If she wanted to be alone, that was all well and good. I'd leave her be and maybe read a book or something. But at this particular moment, with the wind howling and the house groaning against the storm's pressure, I was keen to have a little company. So I got out of bed, slipped on my slippers, and went out onto the second floor landing.

The hallway was almost pitch black. The moon would have usually given it a clean, ashen glow; but tonight, the storm hid all light, and so I stood in the doorway, letting my eyes adjust. At the other end of the hallway was the room we had been planning on turning into a shared study, though for the moment it was mostly being used for storage. Perpendicular to this room was the bathroom. Both doors stood open. Walking on the balls of my feet, I peeked into the study first, then the bathroom. Nothing but darkened shapes, somehow both familiar and foreboding. Olive could be sitting among the maze of stacked boxes in the would-be study, hunkered down in her private mourning. But I didn't think that was the case. It seemed like I would have felt her there.

Walking down the stairs, I glanced out the stairway window. Our pitiful backdoor bulb cast its weak glow against the tempest, a tiny haven of light against the swarming cacophony of night. Without meaning to, I scanned the forest edge, but it was too dark. If anything unnatural moved there—or rather, didn't move—I wouldn't be able to tell.

Olive was nowhere to be found in the living room, though by no means did it feel empty. The bulk of our furniture, indistinct shadows in the gloom, felt strangely alive, as if I had stumbled into some dank cavern, filled with large dozing creatures. I found myself tiptoeing, convinced (for a few brief moments) that they would pounce if I alerted them to my presence. Thunder groaned and lightning lit up the room. Though I saw the couch, armchair, and television, the sense of dangerous occupancy only grew. I stood at the bottom of the stairs, oddly terrified. A small voice in my head told me that those shapes that I had seen *were* creatures who had wandered in from the forest. They were only pretending to be furniture.

The kitchen was no different. I tried the light switch only to find it dead. Odd. The power must have gone out at some point between walking downstairs and entering the kitchen. The wind howled.

"Olive?" I whispered. No response. I scanned the room; there was nowhere else she could be in the house. Unless . . .

My eyes landed on the basement door, opened just a crack. I swallowed.

"Olive," I said again, louder this time. No answer.

I hadn't even seen the basement yet. I knew Olive had stored some things down there, but I had always been spooked by subterranean spaces. People don't belong underground. She wouldn't be down there, would she? It seemed unlikely. Why would she be in the basement while the power's out and a storm's raging?

But there was no alternative: she was in the basement, or she was out in the storm. Thunder crashed, shaking the house, as if to illustrate how unlikely the second possibility was.

I walked to the drawer next to the sink filled with random bric-a-brac from the move and pulled it open. A small green flashlight rolled toward me and I snatched it out, walking to the basement door before I lost my nerve.

The flashlight cast a feeble beam down the wooden steps, revealing a dirty concrete floor.

"Olive?" I called, my voice thin and reedy. I swallowed and tried again. "Olive, are you down there?" Nothing.

I can't say how long I stood at the top of those stairs, but it felt like a very long time. As the storm continued to rage and bellow outside, I considered our predicament. If I'm being totally honest, I was considering *my* predicament. I loved Olive very, very deeply; I was never going to abandon her after all that had happened. The enormity of the loss was too staggering, and it often felt like I was the lone barrier between Olive and oblivion. But since we had arrived in Vermont, a sense of slow strangulation had begun to take hold of me. For all intents and purposes, Olive was absent from my life. I could feel her drifting further away with every passing hour, while I drifted further from the rest of the world. My sense of isolation had grown more and more profound until I found myself staring into my basement, unsure if I was frightened of or frightened for the woman I loved.

But what of it? What of my anxiety, my hurt feelings, my isolation? What was that in the face of what Olive had to endure? Standing at the top of the stairs, staring into the abyssal depths of this strange house, I realized something: I had never fully attempted to understand Olive. Not this new version of her anyway. I had been too preoccupied with protecting her, with keeping her from drifting beyond my reach.

And so, standing at the top of the stairs, I did what I had been afraid to do: I waded into Olive's agony. I took a step, then another, allowing the muted horror of her life to slowly consume me. With each step, I removed another brick from the wall I had erected between us. The blackness swallowed me. I was dwarfed by the scale of her loss. It knocked the wind out of me. By the time I reached the bottom, my breath was shallow and tears streamed down my face.

"Olive?" I croaked. "Please come out, Tini. I'm right here. I'm here now." I swung the flashlight across the dingy interior, revealing cobwebs, rotting cardboard boxes, and rusted pipes. I saw no Olive. I ventured deeper into the basement, around the boiler, into an open space. A small stack of boxes stood in the center, newer than the others. The box on top, labeled "FAMILY" in black letters, was open, the flaps pulled back, reminding me of lolling tongues.

Curious, I stepped closer, pulled back the flap of the box and shined the light inside. I stared for a long time, brow furrowed, tears drying on my face.

Leaves.

The box was full of dead leaves. I reached inside, thinking maybe there was something beneath the collected foliage. But there was nothing. Just leaves, all the way down.

Suddenly, the storm sounded much closer, and a gust of charged, frigid air buffeted against my back. I turned, gasping, but saw nothing. Another gust raised my skin into gooseflesh.

Olive, I thought, but couldn't say why. I ran across the basement and up the stairs, the leaves rustling in my wake.

Back upstairs, the storm had fully infiltrated the house. The wind tossed curtains and photos; detritus from the tempest swirled through the kitchen like miniature storms, newborn babies of the gale. Panic hot in my lungs, I staggered toward the living room, hands held in front of me to protect against the spitting moisture and the natural fury that had pried its way in.

Olive stood at the threshold, one hand placed on the doorframe, gazing out into the night. A shadow moved in the dark beyond the door.

"Olive?" I called. She jumped, then turned to look at me. She threw the door closed with a snap, banishing the storm back into the night. The silence that followed gave me a sense of eerie expectation. "What are you doing?" I asked.

She was soaking wet, rainwater dripping from her hair and nightgown onto the floor. But even in the dark, she looked altered. Her face seemed to glow.

"Enjoying the weather," she said, a smile playing at the corners of her lips.

I stared at her, dumbfounded. She didn't say anything else, just stood there, hands held behind her, like a patient school child waiting to be dismissed. I thought about the box in the basement. Was it possible that grief had finally gotten the better of her? Had Olive passed over some threshold without my noticing?

I sighed. Perhaps she had, but I wasn't going to fix anything right then. Olive shivered and hugged herself, but still didn't move.

"Let's get you in the shower," I said, putting my arm around her. Her skin was cold.

✶✶✶

The next day, Olive woke before I did. The sound of clinking pans brought me from the depths of a strange dream, which dissipated upon waking. I sat up in bed, bleary-eyed and confused. There was another sound among the metallic clatter and scrape of pans. It was so foreign, it took me a moment to place it. When I understood, I pulled the blankets off and went downstairs.

I stood in the kitchen doorway, watching Olive as she made eggs, humming a gentle melody to herself. She didn't notice me right away, and for a while I didn't say anything, content to enjoy the picture before me, strange and unexpected as it was. When she turned to plate the scrambled eggs, she saw me and smiled. It was like watching the sun rise after months of night.

"Good morning," I said, returning the smile. "Nice to see you up so early."

"It's 10:30," she said, her tone sardonic.

My smile widened. She brushed past me and set two plates on the kitchen table, then sat and began to eat with great enthusiasm. I sat across from her, watching her eat, mulling over how best to broach the subject.

"You seem different today," I said quietly. She glanced up from her breakfast, then returned her attention to her eggs. She shrugged. "Did your excursion last night help?"

"Yes," she said, and took a large bite. She didn't seem like she was going to offer any more, so I tried again.

"Olive," I said, and waited for her to look at me. After a few moments of contemplative chewing, she raised her eyes to mine. "Why were you out in the storm?"

She gazed at me for a few heartbeats, searching my face for something. She swallowed and put her fork down.

"You've noticed that this place is different, right?" she asked. The question was so unexpected that I answered without thinking. "Yes," I said.

She looked surprised. "Good. I didn't think you were paying attention." The comment irked me, though I said nothing. This was the most I'd gotten out of her in weeks; I wasn't going to ruin it by being insulted. "Last night," Olive continued, "I woke up, and I thought I heard someone singing out in the storm."

I frowned. "Singing?"

She nodded, then hummed a few bars of the song she had been humming earlier. The melody was odd, almost eerie, full of minor notes and unexpected intervals. I found it strangely soothing, like a half-remembered lullaby from childhood.

"I got up and went to the front door. I could hear the song clearly, even through the closed door. So I opened it." Here, the smile returned to her face, but it wasn't for sharing. It was a smile just for her. "I was scared, at first, because the storm was so wild. All the trees were swaying and shaking. It looked like they were going to be torn from their roots. But there was one tree . . . " Olive shook her head slowly, eyes dreamy. She didn't continue for a long moment. She seemed lost, caught up in the memory, as if living it for a second time. When she spoke again, it was an entirely new thought. "I think I've been looking at it wrong," she said.

"Looking at what wrong?" I asked. A sudden fear had gripped me, and I found that it was difficult to keep my voice steady.

Olive gestured around her.

"All of it, I guess," she said. "I thought I knew how everything worked. I thought I was alone and that what . . . what had happened didn't really matter. That I didn't really matter. It all just seemed random and uncaring." She reached across the table to take my hand. It was warm, as if it had been sitting in sunlight. "I know you care," she said softly. "I see how hard you've been trying. I love you for that. I love you forever for that." She squeezed my hand. "I just need you to know that, okay?" I searched her face. There seemed to be a buried implication in what she was saying, a shrouded ultimatum. A goodbye, maybe? My heart turned to ice at the thought.

"Last night," I said, "I went down to the basement." The warm smile slid from her face, and she retracted her hand. "There was a box. It was labeled FAMILY but . . . but it was just full of leaves. Did you do that?" She gazed at me steadily for a few moments, then stood. She picked up her plate and walked to the kitchen, but not before putting a hand on my shoulder and kissing me on my cheek.

✳✳✳

I woke to the scratching of a tree branch at our window. I lay in the dark, watching with wide eyes as it clicked and skittered across the glass. It seemed to move against the storm wind. A clap of thunder shook the house. I jumped and seemed to lurch out of a waking dream. I rolled over in the darkness, feeling for Olive, already knowing what I would find. Her side of the bed was empty.

I ran downstairs, listening for her, but only hearing the storm, closer than it should have been. I stumbled into the living room and found the front door hanging open, the storm pushing its way in with greedy fingers. I snatched my coat off the rack and ran into the night.

The storm pushed against me like an angry crowd. I could barely see through the rain and darkness. I could hear nothing but the wind howling in my ears.

"OLIVE!" I bellowed, and a crack of thunder answered my call. Lightning lit up the night and I caught a glimpse of trees, jostling and waving, a stampede of giants. I staggered forward. Through the trunks, I thought I saw a flash of white and took off after it.

Branches lashed my face. I felt scratches and bruises forming as trees impeded my path. It felt as if they were trying to push me away, trying to keep me from interfering. Another flash, this time to my left. I turned and took off after her, my heart racing in my chest.

All at once, the trees fell away and I found myself standing in a field. I looked around wildly and spotted Olive at the other end of the field, at the tree line. She had her arms extended into the night. Exultant.

"OLIVE!" I shouted over the roaring of the wind. She looked over her shoulder at me. Even at a distance, I could see her eyes shining.

I took two shambling steps toward her, but then she turned fully toward me and held up a hand. I stopped, horrified and confused, the wind lashing my face, rain stinging my exposed skin like thousands of tiny bullets. Through the chaos, I found Olive's face. Lightning flashed, illuminating half of her features, throwing the other half in even deeper shadow. She was smiling. In the dark, she glowed.

"It's okay," she said. She spoke softly, but the wind caught her words and carried them to me across the field and I heard them as if she had whispered into my ear.

Then, she turned and raised her arms again.

Spell broken, I staggered toward her, slipping and stumbling to my knees in the sodden grass. I cried out and looked up, but she hadn't moved. I stood and resumed running, but stopped about ten yards away, my mouth hanging open, my eyes growing wide.

Olive rose above me, arms still spread, rising to the sky like a balloon made of light. Something held her. Something large and solid with thick arms and gentle fingers. Olive rose until she disappeared into the branches. Leaves cascaded from the canopy, a rain of decay, the shedding of a past self. The tree straightened.

High above me, I saw one black marble eye, large as my head, peer down at me through the veil of rain. It regarded me steadily and without concern, and I felt a sudden rush of calm overtake me. My heartbeat slowed and my body seemed to warm, even in the cold rain. In that moment, I knew I could follow it and Olive into the forest. In that moment, I knew someday I would.

The tree blinked, and then it was moving. I watched it go as it blended into its brethren and disappeared from sight.

Before it did, I thought I heard a sound carried on the storm. I could be wrong, but I could have sworn it was Olive's voice. She was singing. The song was familiar and haunting, a lullaby from my childhood. Or perhaps from before then. Olive vanished into the forest, carried in loving arms, singing a song much older than either of us.

ACKNOWLEDGEMENTS

When I was a kid, I had a dream. I was playing with my friends at the edge of the forest near the house where I grew up. They were all pointing at something hidden among the trees. I got this horrible feeling, a sensation of creeping dread, and I left to go hide in my room. In my room, I laid down on the floor and pressed my back to my bed, which was just a mattress at the time, and waited. Moments later, I heard the sound of sharp nails on my windowpane. And heavy breathing.

This dream has stuck with me my whole life and eventually formed the basis for *The Black Lord*, which is probably why there's so much thematic imagery around the concept of childhood in the piece. I loved those woods near my house, but I also feared them. To me, they represented everything unknown beyond my door, both good and bad. And at night, it seemed as if the trees crept closer to the house, as if they wanted a better look at me.

I have to thank my parents, Tom and Jill Hinckley, for so many things: encouraging my artistic pursuits, teaching me how to be kind and loving, and for raising me at the edge of this forest, which allowed my imagination to expand in ways I don't think it would have in the city. They have been unwavering in their support for me, especially at my lowest, and my gratitude and love for them cannot be properly quantified.

Mariah and Adam, who this piece is dedicated to, are my younger sister and brother, and much of this story stems from early-life anxiety over losing them or not being able to protect them. Turns out they're both tough as nails, and don't really need my protection. I love them both and am extremely proud of both of them.

Next I want to thank the Autumn People—GennaRose Nethercott, Meagan Masterman, and Cassandra de Alba—the best spooky writing group a guy could ask for. I picked *The Black Lord* up after years of neglect during one of our retreats, and their enthusiasm and ideas for the piece gave me the momentum to finish. They realized Laura was possessed before I did! Once more and forever: Blessed be the bones.

Thanks also go to Matt Blairstone and Alex Woodroe at

Tenebrous Press. I'm so grateful for all they've done and I continue to be blown away by the community they've created and the depth of talent they continue to attract. Double thanks go to Alex for her immaculate editing and for understanding *The Black Lord* on a very deep level, in some ways deeper than myself. I feel extremely lucky to be a member of the Tenebrous Cult.

I feel I would be remiss without thanking a few authors who I consider to be my literary grandparents, though all but one have passed on, and will not know my gratitude. But if you like this book, I strongly encourage you to seek them out. First, Algernon Blackwood, whose work lives in the deep roots of *The Black Lord*. Second, Shirley Jackson, whose robust and steady control over the minds of her characters always seemed like a magic trick to me. Third, William Hope Hodgson, whose imagination boggles the mind; I hope to someday make something half as insane as *The House on the Borderland*. And lastly, Stephen King, whose writing brought my writer's brain into screaming consciousness and whose works have been a constant companion throughout my life. Thankee, Sai.

Thanks also goes to Sean Hurley, who read an early draft of the manuscript, though he knew me primarily as an actor. His own work as a writer—especially his play *Food & Shelter*, which I was lucky enough to be cast in—is a source of inspiration for me. He was the one who suggested the title of *The Black Lord,* a choice so obvious in retrospect that I can't believe it was ever anything else.

Thank you also to all my Village Well friends and co-workers who have been uniformly enthusiastic and supportive of me and my work. It's really nice to spend so much time around good people and good books.

Thank you also to the horror community at large which is simply just the kindest and most supportive—and protective—online community that I've ever been a part of. I hope this one scares you all.

And lastly, the most thanks goes to my partner and fiance, Amanda Taylor, whose patience and love and talent make my life exponentially richer than it was before. This book wouldn't exist without her support and encouragement. Her talent as a writer and her insight as a person is invaluable to me and to the world, and before long, everyone else will know it, too. Can't wait to spend the rest of our lives together. Love you, peanut.

Oh, also thanks go to Franklin, though he can't read.

ABOUT THE CONTRIBUTORS

Colin Hinckley grew up at the edge of the forest in rural Vermont where many of his most enduring nightmares were born. His work has appeared in *Tales to Terrify*, *The Lindenwood Review*, and more. He lives in North Hollywood, California with his fiance, Amanda, and his cat, Franklin.

Matt Blairstone is the publisher and founder of Tenebrous Press, as well as a writer, artist and editor. He lives in Portland, Oregon.

Echo Echo is a Portuguese artist and a proponent of *horror vacui*. She immerses herself in individual pieces for up to a year at a time and renders in extreme detail. Echo also performs in multiple bands, finding equal freedom in expressing herself through music as she does through illustration.

TENEBROUS PRESS

aims to drag the malleable Horror genre into newer, Weirder territory with stories that are incisive, provocative, intelligent and terrifying; delivered by voices diverse and unsung.

NEW WEIRD HORROR

FIND OUT MORE:

www.tenebrouspress.com

Twitter @TenebrousPress
Bluesky @tenebrouspress.bsky.social
Join the Tenebrous Cult on Discord

TENEBROUS

PRESS